Gun Boss of Tumbleweed

SELECTED FICTION WORKS BY L. RON HUBBARD

FANTASY

The Case of the Friendly Corpse

Death's Deputy

Fear

The Ghoul

The Indigestible Triton

Slaves of Sleep & The Masters of Sleep

Typewriter in the Sky

The Ultimate Adventure

SCIENCE FICTION

Battlefield Earth

The Conquest of Space

The End Is Not Yet

Final Blackout

The Kilkenny Cats

The Kingslayer

The Mission Earth Dekalogy*

Ole Doc Methuselah

To the Stars

ADVENTURE

The Hell Job series

WESTERN

Buckskin Brigades

Empty Saddles

Guns of Mark Jardine

Hot Lead Payoff

A full list of L. Ron Hubbard's
novellas and short stories is provided at the back.

*Dekalogy—a group of ten volumes

L. RON HUBBARD

Gun Boss of Tumbleweed

GALAXY
PRESS

Published by
Galaxy Press, LLC
7051 Hollywood Boulevard, Suite 200
Hollywood, CA 90028

Printed in the United States of America.

ISBN-10 1-59212-274-4
ISBN-13 978-1-59212-274-5

Library of Congress Control Number: 2007903611

Contents

Stories from Pulp Fiction's Golden Age

A ND it *was* a golden age.

The 1930s and 1940s were a vibrant, seminal time for a gigantic audience of eager readers, probably the largest per capita audience of readers in American history. The magazine racks were chock-full of publications with ragged trims, garish cover art, cheap brown pulp paper, low cover prices—and the most excitement you could hold in your hands.

"Pulp" magazines, named for their rough-cut, pulpwood paper, were a vehicle for more amazing tales than Scheherazade could have told in a million and one nights. Set apart from higher-class "slick" magazines, printed on fancy glossy paper with quality artwork and superior production values, the pulps were for the "rest of us," adventure story after adventure story for people who liked to *read*. Pulp fiction authors were no-holds-barred entertainers—real storytellers. They were more interested in a thrilling plot twist, a horrific villain or a white-knuckle adventure than they were in lavish prose or convoluted metaphors.

The sheer volume of tales released during this wondrous golden age remains unmatched in any other period of literary history—hundreds of thousands of published stories in over nine hundred different magazines. Some titles lasted only an issue or two; many magazines succumbed to paper shortages during World War II, while others endured for decades yet. Pulp fiction remains as a treasure trove of stories you can read, stories you can love, stories you can remember. The stories were driven by plot and character, with grand heroes, terrible villains, beautiful damsels (often in distress), diabolical plots, amazing places, breathless romances. The readers wanted to be taken beyond the mundane, to live adventures far removed from their ordinary lives—and the pulps rarely failed to deliver.

In that regard, pulp fiction stands in the tradition of all memorable literature. For as history has shown, good stories are much more than fancy prose. William Shakespeare, Charles Dickens, Jules Verne, Alexandre Dumas—many of the greatest literary figures wrote their fiction for the readers, not simply literary colleagues and academic admirers. And writers for pulp magazines were no exception. These publications reached an audience that dwarfed the circulations of today's short story magazines. Issues of the pulps were scooped up and read by over thirty million avid readers each month.

Because pulp fiction writers were often paid no more than a cent a word, they had to become prolific or starve. They also had to write aggressively. As Richard Kyle, publisher and editor of *Argosy*, the first and most long-lived of the pulps, so pointedly explained: "The pulp magazine writers, the best of them, worked for markets that did not write for critics or attempt to satisfy timid advertisers. Not having to answer to anyone other than their readers, they wrote about human beings on the edges of the unknown, in those new lands the future would explore. They wrote for what we would become, not for what we had already been."

Some of the more lasting names that graced the pulps include H. P. Lovecraft, Edgar Rice Burroughs, Robert E. Howard, Max Brand, Louis L'Amour, Elmore Leonard, Dashiell Hammett, Raymond Chandler, Erle Stanley Gardner, John D. MacDonald, Ray Bradbury, Isaac Asimov, Robert Heinlein—and, of course, L. Ron Hubbard.

In a word, he was among the most prolific and popular writers of the era. He was also the most enduring—hence this series—and certainly among the most legendary. It all began only months after he first tried his hand at fiction, with L. Ron Hubbard tales appearing in *Thrilling Adventures, Argosy, Five-Novels Monthly, Detective Fiction Weekly, Top-Notch, Texas Ranger, War Birds, Western Stories,* even *Romantic Range.* He could write on any subject, in any genre, from jungle explorers to deep-sea divers, from G-men and gangsters, cowboys and flying aces to mountain climbers, hard-boiled detectives and spies. But he really began to shine when he turned his talent to science fiction and fantasy of which he authored nearly fifty novels or novelettes to forever change the shape of those genres.

Following in the tradition of such famed authors as Herman Melville, Mark Twain, Jack London and Ernest Hemingway, Ron Hubbard actually lived adventures that his own characters would have admired—as an ethnologist among primitive tribes, as prospector and engineer in hostile climes, as a captain of vessels on four oceans. He even wrote a series of articles for *Argosy,* called "Hell Job," in which he lived and told of the most dangerous professions a man could put his hand to.

Finally, and just for good measure, he was also an accomplished photographer, artist, filmmaker, musician and educator. But he was first and foremost a *writer,* and that's the L. Ron Hubbard we come to know through the pages of this volume.

This library of Stories from the Golden Age presents the best of L. Ron Hubbard's fiction from the heyday of storytelling, the Golden Age of the pulp magazines. In these eighty volumes, readers are treated to a full banquet of 153 stories, a kaleidoscope of tales representing every imaginable genre: science fiction, fantasy, western, mystery, thriller, horror, even romance—action of all kinds and in all places.

Because the pulps themselves were printed on such inexpensive paper with high acid content, issues were not meant to endure. As the years go by, the original issues of every pulp from *Argosy* through *Zeppelin Stories* continue crumbling into brittle, brown dust. This library preserves the L. Ron Hubbard tales from that era, presented with a distinctive look that brings back the nostalgic flavor of those times.

L. Ron Hubbard's Stories from the Golden Age has something for every taste, every reader. These tales will return you to a time when fiction was good clean entertainment and the most fun a kid could have on a rainy afternoon or the best thing an adult could enjoy after a long day at work.

Pick up a volume, and remember what reading is supposed to be all about. Remember curling up with a *great story*.

—Kevin J. Anderson

KEVIN J. ANDERSON *is the author of more than ninety critically acclaimed works of speculative fiction, including The Saga of Seven Suns, the continuation of the Dune Chronicles with Brian Herbert, and his New York Times bestselling novelization of L. Ron Hubbard's Ai! Pedrito!*

Gun Boss of Tumbleweed

CHAPTER ONE

Blackmail Job

SOME day, hombre, one of these squeezed-out rancheros is goin' to get past your guns, and when he does, they'll be measurin' you for a sod kimono. And personally, it'll do my heart a world of good to see you skippin' over the red-hot coals of hell."

Mart Kincaid said it with insolence, a wicked flash in his eye. But somehow it was tired, too—tired with the weight of five years on the payroll of Gar Malone, King of the Concha Basin.

The sun was August hot in the searing blue bowl of the Southwest sky, but it wasn't the sun which made Gar Malone jerk his hat lower to hide his eyes.

They sat their horses for a little, on the edge of the trail, neither one of them willing to let it drop without further venom—for they hated each other as the rattlesnake hates the gila, and they had hated each other for a long, long time.

Gar Malone was corpse-thin, hot for gain, killer-ruthless in his sway of range in four hugely unsurveyed counties. His eyes were dark, his teeth were black, there was no light whatever to the flame of thirsty ambition which scorched within him, searing him on to further power, further wealth, further conquest.

He was no coward, Gar Malone, but he knew his man.

"What objections you got? Seems like you're kinda late, Kincaid."

"Sure, sure. I'm the fallen sparrow and my hands ain't fit to touch a decent horse. But they ain't my crimes, Gar Malone."

"Crimes? Why for cripe's sake, what kind of a baby have you turned into? What's criminal in bein' the biggest horn toad in this furnace? What's so damned dirty about shovin' weaklings and peewee stockmen out of the country? Did they invent it? God made it, Kincaid, and it's for the one that can take it and keep it."

"God may have made it," said Mart, "but He sure didn't count on a brand artist comin' along and turnin' it into what it is. There ain't fifty decent people from here to Tumbleweed. It's gettin' kind of monotonous pitchin' into every poor citizen that wants to eat, work and prosper within a hundred miles any direction. I don't object to dirt but I get tired wallerin' in it and pretendin' it's rose petals."

"You goin' to Tumbleweed, or ain't you?" snapped Gar.

"Oh, sure, sure. I'll go to Tumbleweed. I'll knock out the Singing Canyon spread. I'll stand back and let the boys throw lead into honest punchers whose only crime is bein' loyal to a good boss. Sure, I'll do it."

"Now, that's better," said Gar, mollified considerable. "You're the best gun in the state and the gold I pay clinks. But by all that's holy, Kincaid, if I have to go on takin' all this off'n you, you think I'm goin' to forget what I know?"

"Dead men ain't got no memories to speak of at all," said Kincaid.

Gar's dark gaze fastened upon the silver-chased cannons in Kincaid's buscadero belt. His breath went shallow. "Try it, Kincaid. Go ahead and try it. And the Saturday I don't appear in Lawson, Jeb Barly takes the sealed packet out of his bank safe and puts it in the hands of the US deputy marshal. You won't be the only one that will get green-gilled that day. Think twice, gunman. Think twice."

"You ain't panicky, are you?" said Kincaid. His laugh was insolent, without any amusement whatever.

"You think I don't know your fanning? Why do I pay you? And we both know why you go on workin' for me. I need you. You and Gary O'Neil need me alive." Gar's mood changed into pretended lightness and warmth. "I hear," he continued, "that young Gary's ma got herself a new house on her birthday. Now wasn't that just wonderful of you boys? I tell you, it does my heart good."

"You know, hombre," said Mart, "there's times when I just plain itch to let the desert breezes fan gently through yore hide." And as swift as lightning he rolled his guns and slammed four rapid shots into a cast-off canteen beside the trail. The first made it leap into the air, the second, third and fourth rent it apart before it could fall once more.

The first shot Gar had felt in his own flesh. He didn't breathe comfortably until the white powder smoke had drifted well down the trail.

"I guess," said Mart, "that I'll be headin' out for Tumbleweed."

He jerked his pack horse forward and spurred his gray.

If he had looked back he would have seen Gar Malone still sitting his bay beside the trail, looking after him with eyes which sought furtively for a way to end this tension and still rule the Concha Basin.

But Mart Kincaid didn't look back. He was in a more than usually bitter mood. At twenty-five, he felt, he should be well on his way toward making a decent man of himself, carving a fine future from this gaudy but fertile desert realm. But who was he? Gar Malone's peacifier. At twenty-five he was Mart Kincaid, general of the forces of Concha Basin's private and personal devil, a man who used him as guns and brains and kept him chained as thoroughly as Gar's big greyhounds, imported from the East to run down and kill wolves.

It was sixty miles as the buzzard soars to Tumbleweed but it was better than twenty-nine more if one connected with the water holes and used the better trails. But Mart was in no hurry and he added six more in a detour past O'Neil's small ranch.

He felt bad and his eyes were turned so far in that as he came through the canyon below the ranch he did not see, there on the narrow trail before him, the six Malone punchers, part of the home ranch crew.

Johnny Destro saw him and pulled up, halting the others behind him with a half-raised hand. Destro had no love for Kincaid, for Destro considered himself something of a gunner—a fact which he wisely kept to himself. Destro looked at the rangy gray and the slender rider and narrowed his eyes.

Just as Kincaid would have collided with him, unseeing, Destro yanked his reins and climbed the wall.

"Hello, Mr. Kincaid," said Destro, hurriedly assuming a smile.

"Nice day, Mr. Kincaid," said others of the crew.

Mart rode on through them at a brisk trot, packhorse following. The last man in the line saluted with careful carelessness.

"Hiya, Mr. Kincaid."

Mart, aware of the group for the first time, glanced over his shoulder at them and said nothing.

The group dropped uncomplainingly back into the trail and rode on.

Mart leaned out of the saddle and opened a gate. He tied his pack animal there, for he did not intend to linger, and rode on up to the house. Nobody answered his hail and he reined into a gravel path and went out through the garden to the cottage they had built for Gary's mother.

Mrs. O'Neil had the stout heart and proud head of her Irish kings and the sorrows she had experienced were well hidden behind her fine old eyes. Aproned and flushed with the heat of a stove, she came out of the summer kitchen of her small house, carrying an apple pie which she set in the shade to cool.

She didn't see Mart until his jingle bobs sounded immediately behind her and she whirled to find herself hugged.

"Hello, Mother!"

"Mart, you set me down. For shame, you'll have scared the lights out of me! Sneakin' up that way!"

"Where's Gary?"

"He's out with the boys putting some cattle in the south

pasture. That nice Mr. Malone's men brought them up for him. Cut them out of their herd, they did. And that's what I consider as right thoughtful. But come in, come in and sit down and I'll put some weight on you. My, my, Mart, how thin you are! Oh, those ranch cooks. Food spoilers, that's what they be."

"No, Mother," Mart said. "I've got to ride and I may not be back until around the first of October."

"Oh, another one of them special jobs. Mart, I can't see why Mr. Malone can't send somebody else once in a while. He wears you down razor thin, he does. But here. Take this pie. I've got two more and I was just a-thinkin' you might be by. Take it. Now, right in this sack. And mind you don't spoil it."

Mart kissed her and swung back on his gray, pie precariously in hand. He tied it carefully on top of his slicker, right side up, obeying all instructions and then, with a wave, he rode down to the gate.

Gary had seen the pack animal and was waiting, mounted.

They shook hands, no greeting other than that necessary or more expressive. Of the two Mart was the hard, tall one, the leader, and Gary, smaller and softer, was the worshipful follower.

"Malone business?" said Gary.

"Tumbleweed. It's the Singin' Canyon spread this time. Malone says he's tired of water hogs, but the truth is whoever owns Singin' Canyon had the rights filed about thirty years ago when the country was young as a papoose. But it's nothin' to worry about. If I don't do it, somebody will and mebbe with more blood."

"Mart, I'm worried about Mom. Her heart ain't what it was and she had a bad one last night. I can't keep her down. She says if she ain't around doin' what she can she'd plumb waste away. But . . . I smell pie."

"You got two at the house, sonny. Don't sheep-eye mine."

"Can I reach you if anything happens to her?"

"They got a telegraph in Tumbleweed. I'll send a man in every day for mail."

"Thanks, Mart. I don't know what I'd do . . . Well, take care of yourself." He ashamedly shook the emotion away which had been trying to shake his voice.

"You take care of Mom," said Mart. "I'll do the rest."

"Good Mart."

"Adiós."

CHAPTER TWO

Tortured Button

MART hit the trail with no eye for the afternoon mirages and fantastic buttes before him. He cut at the sage viciously with his quirt from time to time and his face was dark with scowling.

After a little he fell to watching his shadow. Once, like any puncher, he'd found considerable to admire about that mounted silhouette, his California hat, his slim shoulders, but that had been when he was a kid and hadn't accumulated a conscience.

"Mart Kincaid, yuh're gettin' black," he muttered.

Morose, he turned to his guns and cleaned them as he rode easily along. When he had finished he restively sought for something else to keep his mind off of it. But his mind wouldn't obey.

He owed Mrs. O'Neil a lot more than he could ever pay. He could go through this and ten times as much for her and Gary. But why should he rebel now? He'd cut this job out for himself.

Gary was her last child. The others, four of them, had died of typhoid seventeen years ago. A month later her husband had been killed by a bronc—thrown and stamped to death. But somehow she had come through. She'd sold most of the ranch, for its size had been beyond her, and set herself the job of raising Gary. And more than that, when Mart Kincaid's parents had passed away thirteen years before, she had taken Mart and raised him as well.

He would always owe her more than he could pay and he should not grudge the debt or fight the price.

Gary, in some ways, was weak. He was older than Mart by three years, and like any border-bred kid, had roamed around and seen what there was to see. And Gary, seven years ago, had seen fit to forget his obligations enough to become friends with a man named Tom Bellows.

Mart had never seen the fellow, but from all accounts he was a tough one. He had thrown his personality over Gary like a saddle blanket and had taught him things no man should know.

Gary had been weak enough to fall for the argument that if he did just one big job he could make his mother wealthy and happy for life. As Mart understood it, they had tackled a mine with five other owl-hoots, and Gary, as advance, had studied the place for the job.

While Gary, his part done, had waited in a nearby town, Tom Bellows and his partners had killed four men in cold blood and run out with twenty thousand dollars in concentrate. Tom Bellows had tried to pay Gary part of his share, but Gary, dismayed at the extent of the crime, had refused to accept anything and had himself barely escaped being killed.

The boy had come home and one night in a nightmare had unwittingly let Mart in on his secret. When Mart questioned him, Gary readily enough swore him to secrecy and confided everything.

For two years they had waited for the matter to be forgotten. They had been convinced they would never hear of it again when Gar Malone had sent for Mart Kincaid.

How Gar Malone had discovered it, Mart could never find out. But for five long years Mart's wits and speed with a gun had been Malone's.

The details were all on file in the bank safe waiting for Malone's death and Gary's execution immediately thereafter. And once when Mart had balked hard, Malone had gone so far as to enter the bank in Mart's presence and ask for the papers.

And Mart had thought of his debt to Mrs. O'Neil and had done the job.

So it had gone for five long years.

And the handsome face of Mart Kincaid had aged treble with every year of it.

He thought of Gary for a while, and for a moment he was tricked into smiling at one of their boyhood escapades. They had put pants and a hat on a young steer and had sent him out to amaze the range. The amazement had consisted of startling the wits out of a herd newly gathered for branding, and stampeding same over ten square miles. For days they had lain quiet and shivered to think what would happen if Mrs. O'Neil discovered the perpetrators of that crime. For it was actually stated around Lawson that whoever had done it ought to be strung up.

And then he thought again of Mrs. O'Neil and rode bitterly on his way.

He was glad enough to travel in the cool of the evening, when it came, for he had started at a somewhat insane hour for a trip across these clustering ranges. He pushed on at a steady clip, pausing only to shift saddle and pack to change mounts, water up, and gnaw away at the pie. Of the last he saved half, for he didn't know what breed of cooking he would get at Malone's Hot Rock headquarters, to which he was traveling.

So big was the basin, so huge were Malone's holdings in it, that in all his time working for the Big M, Mart had never been to Hot Rock. Nor did he have any idea what riders were there or even if he knew them.

Hot Rock was big all in itself. When it got all the water of Singing Canyon it would be bigger. The rancher who had owned Hot Rock had been buried, some years before, after losing a two-year battle, all his stock, one of his kids and his last dime trying to fight the Big M. And now six years later, it was time to take Singing Canyon over.

Money makes money, said the people who did not know, and so no wonder the size of Malone's holdings. Guns take land, said Malone to himself, and ruled supreme.

Thinking about it deepened his hatred of Malone. Knowing the part he had been made to play brought him close to hating himself. And so he rode, through canyons and around buttes and across salt flats and over parched range, until he had come to within twenty miles of Hot Rock. It lacked an hour of dawn and by moonlight he had been able to make time.

But the moon was gone now and the going treacherous. He headed toward a water hole of which he had hopes, then drew up suddenly.

There was a fire burning there, its flames shimmering upon a still pond in reflection. The pungent mesquite smoke lazed in the quiet air.

But the fire had not made him stop. It was the thin grind of agony which had sawed his ears.

Sagebrush masked all but the silhouette of a man raising a quirt and bringing it down. And the scream came swiftly on the crack of the latigo.

However dulled some parts of Mart Kincaid may have been, there was nothing laggard in his actions now. He urged his weary gray forward, straight over the fire, and snatched the quirt as it came up for another blow.

Then he was off his horse and flaming mad. For the target of the quirt was a little kid, not twelve, who lay trussed in the beaten sand.

Two men were there. One had been seated at the fire, and he came up grabbing iron. Mart's hands blurred and thunder tore the gun from the man's hand.

The man who used the quirt was hauling a Winchester out of its boot and had the misfortune to get the sight stuck. A gun barrel took him over his right ear and multiplied the stars.

"What in thunder's the idea?" howled the disarmed man.

"Supposin' you tell me," Mart said grimly, thrusting his guns back into their holsters. "Where I come from they treat buttons some different. But mebbe that ain't where you come from, hombre."

*He urged his weary gray forward, straight over the fire,
and snatched the quirt as it came up for another blow.*

"Yuh busted my hand!"

"I'll bust the other one and even yuh up if yuh like. Take the wrappin's off that kid!"

"Go to the devil!" snarled the wounded man.

His partner stirred and groaned and somehow managed to sit up. He rubbed the side of his head and tried to recall what had happened. Then he saw Mart, saw that no guns were showing, and made a snatch for the Winchester.

Mart's sharp heel came down with a crunch on the reaching hand, then the spur came back and stuck in the man's chin. Mart moved off.

"Yuh dented my rowel," he complained. "For that, mebbe you can untie our small friend."

Mute agony writhed over the second man. And in the diversion, the kid, seeing more than Mart from the ground, screamed: "Look out!"

Mart turned. There had been a third man in that camp, one who had been silent until now. He leaped up from behind a pack where he had been sleeping and shot straight at Mart.

But Mart, already in motion, felt the slug slam into the dust his leap had raised. He came down shooting, and this time he did not take any pains.

The man who had fired stood up straight, looking surprised, then he staggered sideward, tripped on a log, and fell into the fire. Mart flung him off the embers. But there was no use beating out the fire in the man's shirt. He was dead.

"Clear out!" said Mart, with a jerk of his head to the other two.

They looked at him stupidly. One was a thick, shaggy

brute of a man, with long arms and no forehead. It was he who had used the quirt. The other was a beady-eyed rider of indeterminate age, vicious and ill-kempt.

"Clear out!" repeated Mart, barely raising his voice.

The beady-eyed fellow leaned forward, frowning. His glance flitted to the saddled gray and saw the silver-inlaid initials by the renewed leaping of the flames.

"'MK,'" he whispered. And then louder, "'MK!' Oh, good glory! You're Mart Kincaid!"

The shaggy fellow leaped to his feet. He turned white eyes at Mart, and then with hands which shook got a saddle on a bronc and grabbed the hackamore. Leaving his pack behind, he got out of there ten seconds ahead of his beady-eyed partner.

Mart listened to the hoofs fading into the darkness and turned to kneel beside the kid. With the "Kansas toothpick" from his buscadero belt he snicked through the rawhide thongs and laid the bonds aside. He helped the youngster, who was staring at him fixedly, unmindful of rescue or pain, over to the fire to sit down on a log.

"Now let's see about them whip cuts," said Mart. "Seems to me—"

But it was his turn to blink. For this wasn't a boy. It was a girl in jeans and calico shirt, and a pretty little girl at that. She was not more than seventeen, but it was plain to see that before many years were gone she would be leaving a broken-heart trail anywhere she went and would stampede every dance. She was a lovely girl.

"Well?" she snapped. "Do I look like I got warts on my nose?"

18

"Beg yore pardon," said Mart, "but yuh shore ain't got any warts."

She was massaging her wrists. Her riding boots had protected her ankles from the rawhide, but her wrists had been bare and bore thick welts.

The Drakes of Singing Canyon

PROMPTLY Mart got busy. He went to his saddlebag and got one of Mrs. O'Neil's favorite balms. It was made of lard and turpentine and some other mysterious ingredient, but it worked. It worked so well it made the girl cry out, and this confused Mart a great deal.

But she stood it. And when he had some hot coffee down her and had toasted some of the bitter desert night air out of her, he was content that she needed no more than a little sleep to get over her experience. He had come soon enough to prevent real harm being done.

From time to time, from out of the blanket hood, she eyed him strangely.

"What did he say your name was?" she said at last. "Not Mart Kincaid?"

Mart nodded briefly and went on making flapjacks. But when she continued silent he looked up. She had backed off the log and had him covered with the fallen Winchester. Mart blinked, saw the muzzle unwavering and sat back on his heels.

"Yuh're kind of jumpin' at conclusions, ain't yuh?" he said.

"You're Kincaid, Malone's killer!"

"Now, now. It's shore early in the mornin' to have two

gunfights. Supposin' yuh put that bowzer down and come over and eat a flapjack."

"Eat Malone food! Why, by cripes, mister, I'd eat with buzzards first!"

"Don't yuh think that's kind of strong? And for a young lady, too. I'm disappointed, ma'am."

"All right! Say I'm pretty short of gratitude! Say it! But I'm tellin' you here and now, Mr. Gunslinger, I'm ashamed to have met up with you under any conditions whatsoever. And you can run back to your boss and tell him that if he or any more of his comes near Sally Drake or the Singing Canyon, they'll have so much daylight through them they'll look like windowpanes!"

"Such as them waddies that was about to kill yuh?" said Mart wickedly.

This confused her. Her voice faltered a little. "You are Mart Kincaid and you are Malone's killer, ain't you?"

"Yuh mean yuh're not shore?"

She had had her hysterics. "Oh, why do you have to be so darn decent, Mr. Kincaid! You make it pretty tough on somebody when you come and do what you did. I'm supposed to hate you on sight, and I've practiced hating you ever since we heard you were comin' up to take over Hot Rock and run us off the range. And my pop's been shooting tin cans apart until I can't stand the sight of canned peaches anymore. And then you come along—"

She dropped the gun, threw herself on her face in the sand, beat earth with her fists, kicked and cried.

The gun had left him cool, but this was something he hadn't bargained on.

"Come on," he wheedled, trying to lift her. "It's just that yuh're upset after all that ruckus."

"Upset!" she screamed. "Upset? Why wouldn't I be?" And she went off into another storm.

All this was completely beyond Mart Kincaid to remedy and he stood there, feeling bad, looking down at her. If it hadn't been for his preoccupation, some others would not have got so near without his knowing about it.

Firelight glittered on three rifles, each steady and held on him purposefully.

"Up with 'em, cuss yuh!" a hard, mad voice said.

Mart upped with them and his guns were quickly flipped out and dropped.

He winced. He hated to see those guns abused. But he knew his poker. And the people behind those three rifles meant to kill him.

A fourth man, short gun in hand, stepped close before him. It was graying a little in the east and perhaps that increased this one's pallor. But he was a man who looked like he had been through hell. About forty, tall, solid, he impressed Mart as a definitely worthwhile human being.

"I'm Drake of Singing Canyon," he said coldly. "After what yuh did to us this night, we're goin' to give yuh ten minutes—"

"Pa! Pa, that ain't him!"

The men stared at the girl, who sprang into Drake's arms and began to cry again, and for the first time, Drake saw the dead man Mart had tugged behind a bush. This sudden turn made them uncertain.

"Who are you?" demanded Drake.

"He's Mart Kincaid!" cried the girl. "And he shot them up and made them run and he killed one and just when they were going to whip me! You don't dare touch him!" And she threw herself from her father and shielded Mart.

Mart gently set her aside.

"Mr. Drake, whoever stole this girl—"

"They shot her hoss," said Drake bitterly. "And they killed Luke when he turned on 'em. We found Luke and we've followed this trail ever since sundown when it happened. They doubled on us twice and used water once, but we wasn't half an hour behind 'em. We heard shots and finally saw the fire. And I guess we owe yuh an apology, though givin' an apology to Malone's gun is just about all I can stomach."

"Thanks," said Mart. "That's mighty white of yuh to say so. And now, if you gentlemen don't care to argue the matter any further, I'll crawl leather and be on my way."

"Now wait a minute," protested Drake. "I guess I was pretty hasty, and I've got no right to be after what yuh did for Sally. Here, accept my apology and my thanks and shake on it."

Mart looked at the extended hand, then he gathered up the reins, preparing to mount.

"Mr. Drake," he said, "there's nothin' I'd like better than to be yore friend. But I can't shake hands with yuh."

Drake flushed, and quickly jerked his hand back.

"Why not? By the eternal—"

"I can't because I have to work for Malone. Mebbe I don't

like it, but I work for him because I've got to. I came up here to make trouble for the Singin' Canyon spread and to run you off yore water. Bein' no bushwhacker, that's my warnin'. And that's why I can't shake hands."

Mart swung into saddle and its creak was loud in the stillness. The girl touched his knee and started to protest.

"Miss Sally," said Mart, "yuh're plumb welcome to whatever favor yuh think I might have done for yuh, and it don't need no payment and no thanks. For yore sake I'm goin' to be just as peaceful up here as man'll allow. So keep yore thanks and next time stay on the home range. *Adiós,* gentlemen."

As he picked up his packhorse lead rope he heard one of Drake's men say heatedly: "Why the devil can't I plug him? He'll make more trouble than any of us can handle!"

And he heard Drake say, "There's two reasons, Thorny. One is that I owe him a favor, and two is that he's Mart Kincaid, and yuh'll never live to fire the second shot. Now dig a hole for that dead'n and let's get home." He picked up a quirt and looked at it a moment. "Yuh said somebody tried to whip you, Sally. Why?"

"To write a note to you. I don't know about what. A big hairy brute took the quirt and beat me. And he'd have done worse if Mr. Kincaid hadn't come."

Drake looked thoughtful.

"Was a time Concha Basin was plain paradise. But that was before the devil moved in. I'd like to take a quirt to Gar Malone!"

Sally was looking pensively through the red dawn in the direction Mart had taken.

25

"I wish," she said with apparent irrelevance, "that I was eighteen!"

But it wasn't irrelevant to her father.

"Sally," he said soberly, "whatever he did for you, that man belongs to Gar Malone and it's goin' to be our painful duty, before the year gets much older, to blast Mart Kincaid and his crew out of the desert. And we'll do it. So keep yore hair ribbons stowed in yore war bag. He ain't, and never will be, for you."

Mart Kincaid, however, was not doing Sally Drake any similar compliment of thought. He was more worried than before, and as he rode he came to the conclusion that he was on the wrong track and had been for five years. He was getting older and his hands were getting dirtier.

Drake of Singing Canyon was a fine man. The time was long past when Mart could claim such as a friend. His partners now could be only outlaws, gunhawks, down-at-the-heels punchers, and the spineless gentry who lived off the likes of Malone. Realizing that fact cut him sharply.

That conclusion bode no good for the crew at Hot Rock. Mart Kincaid rode into the grove of pines which shielded and cooled the headquarters and roamed his eyes to take in the condition of things.

CHAPTER FOUR

Kincaid, Gunslinger

ALL was neat and orderly and properly done in a careless, heartless sort of way at the Hot Rock headquarters. That was how it always was with people like Malone. They wanted efficiency. Brass and money could bully men into giving efficiency.

Such huge holdings often ran all too well, sometimes working and improving things far beyond the capacity of small spreads. If a man wanted men to be machines, then the proper system was Malone's. But if a man wanted men to be strong and happy, filled with independence, self-reliance and dignity, then Malone's was exactly and precisely the last way a man should choose.

Saddles neatly pegged, cavvy sleek within an excellent corral, blacksmith shop sparking and clanging, wagons well painted, haying gear neat and oiled, storage houses, bunkhouses, cookhouses and foreman's shack all in a neat quadrangle. And the odor of fresh hay and pine needles sharp and sweet in the air. In truth, Hot Rock was a model spread, complete with rotated ranges, artesian wells, a small irrigation project and good buildings.

Wisdom had been bought and invested here. No Texas fever, all poison feed grubbed out for miles around, the finest shorthorns which could be bought and bred. Once the place had been rickety and wild and run haphazard by a Texan and his five tall sons. It had not been so profitable, but it had served to make men happy—which was more than it was doing now.

A wrangler laid down a riata he had been braiding and came forward into the patched sunlight. Mart threw him his reins and handed over the led horse.

"Kincaid," he said briefly.

The wrangler instantly straightened and looked respectful. "Yes, sir, Mr. Kincaid. Yuh'll find Thompson over in the office. . . . Rub 'em down and oats?"

"Not too many oats," said Kincaid. "Cut me out two good mustangs. I may want to cover a lot of country today."

"Yes, sir, Mr. Kincaid," repeated the wrangler, and looked wonderingly at Mart's departing back.

He was a kid, the wrangler, and he didn't care much yet who he worked for. He hastened with the horses down to the blacksmith shop.

"Things are about to pop, Smitty," he called in. "Mart Kincaid just lit."

The blacksmith stopped hammering. He stood dripping sweat on a hot horseshoe where it went *spit, spit, spit* in small puffs of steam. The muscles of his huge bronze arm twitched spasmodically. He was better than six foot four, and weighed two-forty, and his sun-bleached hair was startling against the grimy burn of his skin.

He put down his hammer and fished a bandana from under his apron, wiping his face. They called him "Boot Hill" Smitty behind his back, Smitty to his face. He had given two men at Tumbleweed an even break and had killed them both. He had a dangerous eye and it told no lies. He was savage, sadistic and never knew when he was hurt.

The kid looked at him in amazement. He had never seen Boot Hill Smitty upset by anything before.

"Get the devil out of here," growled Smitty.

The wrangler went, and had another addition to his gossip when he passed the boys working the hay.

Caring nothing for any impression he might make, Mart kicked open the door of the office. It was a small cubicle in the front of the shack where the foreman lived, and here "Bat" Thompson was finishing up his tallies.

"I'm Kincaid," said Mart.

Bat Thompson spun around in his chair and blinked. Then he hastily got up and spoke with a sudden note of relief.

"Oh. Yuh come up here about Singin' Canyon, didn't yuh? Yuh taking over the whole spread?"

"Keep yore job for the moment." Mart came in and sat down on the desk, swinging one chapped leg slowly while he built himself a smoke.

"What's the matter, Thompson?" he drawled. "Yuh got a guilty conscience?"

"Me?" Bat laughed. "Shucks, no. I just—well—"

Mart spun his match at the tally book.

"Mebbe that don't tell the right tale?" he suggested.

"Oh, no! I mean, of course. It's just a surprise, that's all."

"What is?"

29

"Why, seein' it was you."

"Why should I give yuh indigestion?" asked Mart.

"Look, Kincaid, I been doin' what I could for Malone. I got this place in pretty good shape. Of course we're short of water. Got more grass than we have drink or we'd show a better profit. But this Hot Rock is all right as she is, and the herd we just threw out will make plenty at the current price of beef."

"Put it in a letter to Malone," said Mart. "I didn't come up here to dry-gulch yuh. It's Singin' Canyon. Or at least it was."

"What do you mean by that?" said Thompson.

Boot Hill Smitty spoke from the door. "Yuh got a minute, Thompson?"

"Meet Mart Kincaid, Smitty. Smitty's our blacksmith."

Boot Hill Smitty stood squarely in the door and his small, hard eyes dared Kincaid.

"Howdy," Mart said diffidently.

Smitty sighed and relaxed. "Seein' yuh're busy, Thompson, I'll save it for some other time."

Thompson watched him go. "Now what was all that about?"

"Givin' the new arrival the eye," said Mart. He stood up. "That's how it is, Thompson. You keep things goin', but I'm to take charge of whatever I think best." He received Thompson's nod and started to leave. He turned at the door. "And run it straight while I'm around. All the money I make out of Malone I make as pay, and I expect to stay clean on that score."

"Shore!" said Thompson, with relief. "Oh—yuh can take Malone's shack. He always builds one and never uses it."

30

"That's right hospitable of yuh," said Mart. "Yuh just get back to work."

Mart found the owner's quarters back in the grove. Malone liked to do things in style and he had a theory that so long as there was some symbol of him around, men would knuckle under. And so he had built quarters here and there through his ranches, one at each principal headquarters, and while it was doubtful if he had seen Hot Rock in half a dozen years, the place was well kept and ready for him.

The shack which Thompson occupied was strictly a stable compared to this. A shady veranda, flanked by pines, led into the main room of the L-shaped *casita*. Here was a fireplace of colored stone with a fire carefully laid on the hearth. Here were Navvy rugs of great brilliance, and silver saddle ornaments and an old needle gun for effect. Everything which went to make a home was here, and yet there was a coldness about it, a precise, unlived-in atmosphere which made Mart sigh.

"For a place like this," he murmured, stretching himself in a deep leather chair, "a man could dare an awful lot." He looked around at the mounted heads and grinned with bitter humor. "What? No mounted humans? Malone didn't indulge his delicate taste to the limit after all."

A board creaked behind him. Only at times like this did Mart come fully awake to what he had become. He had whirled back, guns drawn and starting their spin, before he recognized the caller. It was Smitty and the guns didn't scare him any.

"I need iron," Smitty said. "I got to go into town."

Mart holstered his guns and put his thumbs in his belt.

"How long do yuh think yuh'll stay healthy cat-footin' up on growed men from behind, Smitty?" he asked.

"I get along."

"So'll yore soul, if any," said Mart. "Take such things up with the foreman."

"He got a wire yestiddy sayin' you was comin' as manager and to turn over the spread to yuh. How'd I know?"

"Why, shucks, Smitty, you seem to know most everything, don't yuh? Now get out, and the next time knock. Good and loud."

The dangerous eyes flicked like bits of flint. Smitty turned his bulk to the door and walked heavily and loudly away.

"Smitty!" Mart called.

"Well?"

"Yore short gun is showin'."

The blacksmith turned darkly red and fumbled with the weapon which he had hastily secreted in the heavy pocket of his apron.

Mart slammed and locked the door. He found that the wrangler had dumped his pack in the bedroom and he fished out some soap and a towel with which to remove the alkali of travel.

While he was washing in the unused pantry, the cook knocked, and was let in with a tray of steaming chuck. He was a bland-faced Chinese, his only sign of apprehension showing in the rattle of the cups.

Mart sat down to eat. "Tell everybody I'll see 'em in here in half an hour," he said.

The Chinese nodded briskly and got out.

There was steak and potatoes and raisin pie, and Mart ate it all, rather amazed at how hungry he had been. He had finished and was rolling a cigarette when he heard men on the veranda. He called them in and watched them lazily as they sought uncomfortably for positions along the wall. None of them dared sit down.

Thompson started to introduce them, but Mart cut him off.

"The only men I'm interested in can sling lead," he said. "And that ain't the whole crew. Peaceful gents can leave right now and give up the ten-spot bonus that's bein' offered this month."

CHAPTER FIVE

Gun Crew

ODDLY nobody withdrew. Mart looked at the men lined up against the wall with some interest. They were a hard-bitten outfit, down at the heels most of them, tough all of them. He wondered for an instant how many had records in some other part of the West.

"Our three best men ain't showed today," said Thompson uneasily. "Malone's been recruitin' and these hombres is it. Me, all I know is raisin' cattle, and the day this is settled and I can get me some rope hands, fair enough. The boys know what yuh're plannin' to drop a loop on. What they want to know is when."

"Smitty ain't here," said the wrangler.

"He's goin' to town for iron," said Mart. He looked at the kid and wondered what a clean younker like that was doin' in this questionable society. "What's yore name, kid?"

"Brazos," the young wrangler said promptly, thumping his gun.

"Well, Blazos, bring my mustangs around here, and two for yourself. Vamoose." And when the kid was gone he said, "Rest of you gents is ordered to keep workin' and let peace reign. This fight—"

"I come up here for war," said a beefy gunhawk, shifting

his belt. "And if there ain't no war, I'm ridin'. My hands is wore plumb through on that danged pitchfork."

"If yuh're through interruptin'," said Mart, "I'll finish by sayin' that this fight begins when and if I give the word, and agin whoever I indicates, and them as makes trouble for anybody before that, whether Singin' Canyon or a coyote, can talk it over with me, smoky-like. Meetin's adjourned."

They shuffled out, but Thompson lingered.

"Kincaid," he said, "I'd feel better if I just got my time. The Tumbleweed bank has all the funds, and . . . I been runnin' things peaceful here for nine years, and I kind of got a likin' to keep on livin'. Drake's brung in gunfighters and this ain't no picnic in prospect."

"Never met a man so proud of bein' yeller," said Mart coolly. "Throw the account books in here when yuh leave—whatever yuh got—and make dust."

Thompson squirmed and twisted his hat. "Yuh won't—wire Malone I'm leavin'?"

"Thompson, Gar Malone probably has forgot yuh're even livin'. Vamoose."

There was relief in the man as he left, and Mart sat there quietly smoking a quirly until he heard the wrangler. He went out and took his saddled mustang. The kid would have talked volubly, but Mart shut him up with a glance and rode away.

The mustang had been on oats. Not eight hundred pounds, he had a big barrel and short, distance-punishing legs. With the led horses flying behind the wrangler in the dust, Mart headed out toward the disputed water holes.

He went five miles as the bullet flies, down gulches, across mesas, up avalanching banks, riding out some of the cussedness which was in him. And then he swerved without explanation to the wrangler and started off to the north at the same killing pace.

When he came to a trail which was obviously between Hot Rock and Tumbleweed—which town was smally distant in that brilliant air—he located a large boulder, dismounted, and waited for the wrangler.

Brazos came up, pouring sweat, on a white-splashed horse. He looked at the boulder, saw that it was covered from the trail, and dropped off.

"Bushwhack?" he asked.

"Shift saddles, kid."

Mart went up on top of the rock and covertly looked up and down the trail. He slid back and casually squatted on his heels, building a quirly.

"How come yuh decided to go bad, kid?"

Surprise lit up the fresh pink face of the wrangler. He didn't answer.

"Yuh're on the wrong fork," said Mart. "Yuh ever done anything they'd want yuh for?"

"Well—"

"Meanin' no! Kid, while yuh got time, forget about the excitement of smokin' men down and stealin' bread from kids, and live that yore mother'd be proud to tell about."

Brazos stood uncertainly, but the talk had started the wheels going and he turned hastily to hide a glistening tear.

"You shut up," he muttered.

"What's the matter, kid?"

Brazos gulped and faced him. "Yuh leave me alone, dang yuh! I'll do what I please!"

"I suppose that's what your ma'd want."

"Leave me alone!" Brazos yelled at him, then suddenly sat down on a rock and began to cry. He shook off Mart's hand and, left to himself, finally quieted down.

After a while he said, "My ma's dead, Mr. Kincaid. My pop and her worked theirselves to death tryin' to make a livin' on Little Gravelly. There warn't no water to speak of and it wouldn't raise a rattlesnake. I came away three years ago. And if workin' hard done all that to 'em, it ain't for you to tell me to go straight. The only gents I ever seen with money was also packin' guns. I'm sorry, Mr. Kincaid."

Mart had been somewhat taken aback, and he was sorry he had pushed in where no fool would have tread.

"Beg yore pardon, kid."

"And if yuh're so free with advice, why don't yuh—"

"Hush. We got company."

Mart walked out from behind the boulder and into the trail. He laid a casual hand upon the bridle of the red saddler and looked bleakly into the face of Bat Thompson.

Thompson went white and began to shake. He didn't have the nerve to run. He sat there, clutching the lead ropes of his three pack animals, terror pounding in his throat, getting sick.

"Get down," said Mart.

Thompson got down.

With expert fingers Mart frisked him and drew out a thick sheaf of papers. A bankbook fell to the trail and, when examined, proved to be Thompson's personal account. It totaled forty-seven thousand dollars.

"Pretty good for nine years," said Mart. "What'd yuh say Malone paid yuh?"

Thompson made three attempts to answer and finally succeeded. "Hundred and ten a month."

Mart scratched with his finger in the sand. "Seems as how some thirty-five thousand of this belongs to Malone, allowin' that yuh never spent a cent for yoreself all this time. Mount up, Brazos. We're goin' into town with this gent."

The kid brought the horses, turning the spent ones loose to go home by themselves.

"Yuh'll draw it all and give me thirty-five thousand, one hundred and twenty in cash."

"So that's it!" cried Thompson in sudden anger. "Yuh're no better than me!"

Mart smiled slowly. "Thompson, yuh're the first man in some time that's seen fit to give me such an insult. Why don't we get down now and settle this thing man to man?"

"I was jokin'. I was jokin', honest I was! Look here, Mr. Kincaid, can't yuh take a joke?"

"Well, ha, ha. Let's get along, Brazos. You ride in front, Thompson. It's too hot this time of day to go chasin' yuh."

They trotted briskly into Tumbleweed and found the 'dobe town drowsing in the heat. A few dogs got out of the street to let them go by and a Mexican woke up, yawned, and went back to sleep.

Mart dismounted before the bank and genially escorted

Thompson inside. Only the cashier was present, so Mart had no chance to inquire into any further arrangements from the president. The cashier winced at the size of the check.

"Today?"

"Give me a personal receipt as though I deposited thirty-five thousand of that," said Mart, "and this gent will take the rest."

"Good," said the cashier, relieved. "Who to?"

"Mart Kincaid."

The cashier looked at him hard, blinked, then made haste to finish the transaction. Thompson stood numbly while his sum was counted out. He made no sign of protest when Mart pocketed the receipt.

Thompson wanted to go to the general store and get supplies for a trip and Mart sent Brazos along.

"He ain't to talk to nobody," Mart instructed. "Shoo him on his way with my blessin' when he's through."

There was a big sorrel standing before the Golden West Saloon, and Mart eyed the brand. It was an entwined "S" and "C" and Mart brightened. Drake would be somewhere around.

But he had no chance to look for Drake. People dived out of the front of the Golden West and sudden silence settled inside the place.

Gingerly Mart sidestepped through the swinging door, walking light, and backed the wall. Old man Drake was standing at a poker table, while at the bar Johnny Destro, half drunk, was playing with him.

"Go on, draw," growled Destro. "Go on, tough man from

Singin' Canyon. Draw. Look! No hands." And he hid them behind his back.

Mart recognized Malone's home-ranch foreman. Johnny Destro was pretty good with a gun.

"Go ahead," said Mart suddenly. "Draw, Mr. Drake. I don't think he's got enough Hickok in him to try two shots at once. Or have you, Johnny?"

The shock of this made Johnny Destro's jaw sag foolishly. He was trying to argue away the actual import of Mart's words.

"You sidin' with this buzzard, Kincaid?" he asked suddenly.

"My meat, Johnny. You trot along and do whatever Malone sent yuh up here to do. My show has only got one boss and that's me. Now get 'fore I let some air out of yuh. And it is air, ain't it, Johnny? Go on! Tell these gents it's air."

Johnny Destro carefully kept his hands away from his guns. He had told himself several times that he was just as good as Kincaid. He hadn't won the argument.

"It's air," he said bitterly.

Stiff-legged, he walked past Mart and into the street. The door swung back and forth, then settled to a stop. Mart walked to the bar and threw away Johnny's drink.

"Sterilize the glass and give me and Drake a drink," said Kincaid.

"Wait a minute," said Drake behind Mart. "I don't know that I care to drink. Just because yuh bluff out a Malone gunner for me is no reason."

Mart shrugged. "Put the second one away, barkeep. You and me can stand to be alone."

41

CHAPTER SIX

Three Days Late

SADNESS was in Mart Kincaid's eyes as he watched Drake leave the saloon. Two Singing Canyon riders came pounding up, late for the play. They would have come in but Mart heard Drake say:

"Kincaid's in there. Stay out of his way. When the shootin' begins, we'll need all our bullets."

"You takin' this layin' down?" said one.

"I'm startin' it," said Drake.

Leather creaked as they mounted. Mart suddenly remembered he had business with Drake, but when he got to the street the three were well on their way.

Brazos was there with the horses.

"I hear yuh bluffed a Malone gunhawk," the kid said. "What kind of a show is this anyway, Mr. Kincaid?" There was puzzlement on his young face, but admiration, too.

"All aboard for home," growled Mart.

He had started to mount when a cry reached him from the store. Sally Drake was there, helping two punchers load supplies into a spring wagon, while a third sat on the tailgate with a sawed-off shotgun in hand. Mart looked down the road. A few hundred yards out of town Drake and his men were waiting for the rest of their outfit.

"Mart Kincaid!" cried Sally. "Come here!"

The name made the three punchers stiffen and the shotgun come level. Mart ignored them. He mounted and guided his horse over to the walk which was high enough to put Sally level with him.

She had ignored the necessity of rest to make this weekly trip for supplies, and she was all tricked out in divided buckskin skirt, small boots, John B. and a crisp, crinkly blouse. Her hair was fluffed and Mart realized with an abrupt shock that this girl was a beauty indeed. Four years or so and she'd really rock this range.

She gave him a saucy smile. In her hand she held a glittering bit of silver.

"You left this behind, and I do believe it's part of your *barbiquejo.*"

He felt of his chin thong and found the ornament gone. He smiled at her and took it.

"It was bent, but I fixed it," she said, head cocked on one side, beaming at him.

Mart dissolved with the smile. "I shore am obliged. Wondered all day why this knot kept slippin'. Don't know what I'd do without you, Miss Sally."

He had difficulty in restoring the ornament, and she jerked his hat off and put it properly in place.

"There," she said. "Don't know how some men get along without a woman to look after them."

"They mostly don't," said Mart smiling. "Some man's goin' to be mighty lucky someday."

She blushed and it made her prettier. "*Some* man!" She shoved his hat at him.

"Mr. Kincaid!" yelled Brazos.

Mart whirled to see Johnny Destro on the steps of the telegraph office. Johnny underwent a considerable change of color and began to shake.

"Just walk on down the street," said Mart. "And put that peashooter away. It might go off and deprive yuh of a little pink toe."

Johnny had not drawn all the way. He had lost his nerve. He hastily walked as directed and kept on walking even when reason told him that Mart was well on his way.

Mart bowed to Sally, replaced his hat and trotted away. The man with the sawed gun fumed impotently.

"Yuh danged little brat!" he gritted. "Yore ma is goin' to tan yore hide for yuh. I'll see she does. Takin' up with gunmen, gettin' good men kilt."

"Dry up, Jake," said another man. "I couldn't get up my nerve to shoot him in the back neither."

Mart kept his eyes steadily to the front and cheerfully ate up distance homeward. He broke into a whistle now and then until, having dismounted before his temporary home, he suddenly asked himself why. And for the life of him he couldn't answer.

He put Brazos to work sitting on the veranda whittling and watching the road and buildings, and the Hot Rock outfit had to impress another man into tending cavvy.

All evening Mart went over the books and found them to be the most remarkably accurate cheats he had ever inspected. Mrs. O'Neil had taught him considerably more than plain arithmetic, and yet for the life of him he couldn't discover Thompson in any errors or outright fraud. It became obvious at last that Bat Thompson had been a very smart crook indeed, and needed only a little more nerve to rank right with Malone himself.

The puzzle was in the tallies, for it seemed like every single cow that had ever come into the world on Hot Rock had been duly accounted for. Not until midnight did he suspect the truth. Bat Thompson had made it on the men's food and in false vouchers. But the old crew was scattered wide now, and the chances were they did not even know they had been systematically robbed.

Satisfied, Mart rolled in and went to sleep, listening to the kid's snores in front of the living-room door. . . .

Much refreshed, Mart set about inspecting the ranch in the morning and was much interested. He had never seen a spread as hopefully situated nor as pleasantly promising of a rich future.

Riding far, he inspected the water holes in question and was turned back by barbed wire and a random slug to warn him off. And he came to the conclusion that Malone had gone range hog in earnest. For those water holes were not entirely necessary for the prosperity of the Hot Rock. The whole Singing Canyon outfit, if added to the Hot Rock, would take in the valley entire and make this a small empire of itself. The thing was a grab, with a water hole as the flimsy alibi.

Mart kept the gunmen working against their thinly hidden dislike of labor. In the next five days they caught up all the accumulated odds and ends which the regular five-man crew had not had time to accomplish.

He was alert to a possible attack from Drake, for he did

not think the old man's patience would stretch forever after the obvious move Malone had made sending Mart up here, and then, for some peculiar reason, Johnny Destro as well. Accordingly, he bade the men sleep light, with guns to hand, but he saw no reason whatever to set up a watch besides Brazos, who proved to be a light sleeper.

On Saturday evening Brazos came back from an errand which had taken him through some risky territory. Mart was glad to see the kid with a whole skin, for he had sent him with a note to Drake.

Brazos threw some mail contemptuously on the table.

"Stopped through town comin' home," he said, hoping that Mart would not smell his breath or question the fact that town was ten miles out of the way. "Old man Drake give me this for yuh. Them rannies won't fight," he added. "I rid my hoss right up on the front porch and threw yore offer at 'em and they took it sweet's yuh please. They won't fight."

Mart failed to note that Brazos was reeling a little. He was too hopeful of the note. It read:

Kincaid,

I don't see buyin'. Thirty-five thousand wouldn't touch my headquarters for you. If you think this will put us to sleep, come on over and start the ball. You'll find us waiting.

Drake

Mart looked downcast and then, turned grim, he inspected the handwriting and the wording. It showed, he thought, something of emotional stress beyond its bravado, and the fact made him nervous.

A year or two ago he would have taken his wrath out in powder smoke and the devil with it. But that wasn't now. He was sick through and through of dirty work and Gar Malone. If Drake had let him pull this trick, he could have gone back to Lawson with a clean conscience. But now it was different.

He crumpled the note into a ball and threw it at the fire.

Brazos steadied himself against the door, turned carefully, and went out. He found his blankets, got one boot off, covered his head, and started to go to sleep. Something crinkled and he recalled the telegram. For an instant he tried to focus on it and get up, then he recalled that the wire had already been in Tumbleweed two days. Morning was soon enough. And so he snored, sleeping heavily and deeply for once.

Not so Mart Kincaid. The note had shattered his last hope of holding Gar Malone in stalemate. He couldn't be so danged smart, he told himself, to take five years to get sick of a rotten job. Must have a Swede in his ancestry. If he could just quit!

But no, if he didn't effect the combination of the Hot Rock brand and the SC, Gar was liable to do something drastic to Gary O'Neil, for Mart of late had more than suspected that he was not the only one who had tired of the combination.

When he had been a hot-eyed kid, with no more to recommend him than ambidextrous sudden death, Gar had felt certain of his ability to control him. But that was years back now, and he might well appear to Malone as welcome as a halter-broke rattler with a grudge.

What was he going to do? If he couldn't tame the SC, Malone would try pressure, and under pressure, Mart was liable to get irrational with his triggers. And then, sure, Gary O'Neil would be walking up the thirteen steps.

Without any real idea of going anywhere he took up his hat, brushed his hand across the top of the lamp and went out into the star-spotted night. The wind felt cool on his hot cheeks and he stood leaning against the veranda railings, idly counting the blazing stars of Scorpio.

Brazos was moaning and twisting in his sleep, perhaps subconsciously disturbed by the presence of another on the porch. He muttered, and began to thresh out with his fists, and then came up sitting in a knockout war with his blanket. He solidly smashed it with his fist and overswung to connect with the railing. The pain of that brought him wide awake, dazed and uncertain.

"Who's that?" he said suddenly.

"Kincaid. What's the matter, kid?"

"Gee, yuh scared me for a minute. Ugh! What a dream *that* was!"

He gathered himself together, located the makings and built himself one. His face was drawn in the flare of the match.

"Mister," he said, "if a hangin' is as bad as that dream, remind me never to go see none."

The subject startled Kincaid. "Who got hung, son?"

"How should I know? But he made a awful fight of it, let me tell a man. And . . . Yeah, that's what. You come in through the mob and started shootin' everybody in sight, tryin' to cut the gent down, and yuh looked square at me and said, 'Yuh're next, Brazos,' and just 'fore yuh pulled the trigger I woke up. Say, that's timin' it lucky, huh? Another ten seconds of sleep and mebbe I'd be stone dead, drilled clean."

It made Kincaid nervous. "Go to sleep, kid."

Brazos threw away the smoke and started to settle himself again when suddenly a crinkle of paper brought him upright.

In a guilty voice he said: "I forgot to give yuh this, Mr. Kincaid."

Mart took the telegram, and the second he saw it he knew what it contained. By the light of a lucifer he read:

MART THEY GOT ME CLEAN. COME SHOOTIN'.

GARY O'NEIL

The match burned him. He threw it down and went into the house. The telegram was three days old and, for all he knew, Gary was three days dead!

CHAPTER SEVEN

Wild Ride

ANGER made hard ridges on either side of Mart's lean jaw. He swore futilely. He could guess at what had happened now, but he couldn't be sure. And Lawson was eighty-nine miles away!

"Brazos!" he called. "Saddle one and two to lead. I'm on my way."

Brazos came out of it and went off the porch running. Mart tossed his pack together and by the relighted lamp made a thorough inspection of his guns and his rifle. He filled the empty loops in his buscadero belt, and caught up his war bag to find Brazos already there and waiting.

He mounted and saw the kid's white face below him in the starlight.

"Look, Brazos. Here." He got out a stub of pencil and an old envelope and scribbled in the dark. He handed it over. "That puts you in the say-so here and what yuh do, yuh do in my name. My orders are not to do much and not to know anything. If Smitty comes back, fire him for takin' leave without askin', and if Drake turns up tell him to get tight and mebbe this will come out fine for him after all."

"Goodbye, Mr. Kincaid," said Brazos.

"Why that? I'll be back."

Mart swung out, yanked the led horses, dug spur and thundered down the trail.

It is doubtful if anyone else in the Concha Basin ever bettered that ride. For Mart used up two of the horses for keeps and lathered the third one white. He put eighty-nine miles behind him as if they'd been bullets, not heat-scarred, rocky, dangerous desert terrain.

So high was his tension, so deadly his purpose, that he hardly knew how much of himself he had used up. His only notice of his speed was a growl of satisfaction on arrival at the Diamond M home ranch, to see that the sun was not an hour high.

He sat there on his lathered black, looking at the shut blinds of Gar Malone's office. There was thick dust on the threshold. It had not been disturbed for days.

Something like a letdown hit him for an instant, then he either heard or felt the menace around the bunkhouse and whirled, guns drawn, to see Johnny Destro looking down a Winchester's sights. Ten feet to the right of Johnny another gunman had a Colt half drawn.

Winchester and Mart's rolling guns thudded as one. The crown of Mart's hat ripped and the jerk of his head spoiled his third and fourth shots. The gunman with the Colt got in two shots, both of them being fired as his knees buckled, both of them hitting only sky. The man was dead before he hit dirt.

Johnny Destro lowered the Winchester casually. He was leaning straight up against the jamb of the bunkhouse door.

STORIES from the GOLDEN AGE

☐ **Yes, I would like to receive my FREE CATALOG** featuring all 80 volumes of the *Stories from the Golden Age Collection* and more!

Name

Shipping Address

City   State   ZIP

Telephone   E-mail

Check other genres you are interested in: ☐ SciFi/Fantasy ☐ Mystery ☐ Action/Adventure

FREE SHIPPING!
NO PURCHASE REQUIRED

10 Books • 20 Stories
Illustrations • Glossaries

10 Audiobooks • 20 CDs
20 Stories • Full color 40-page booklet

Fold on line and tape

IF YOU ENJOYED READING THIS BOOK, GET THE WESTERN COLLECTION AND SAVE 25%

BOOK SET	AUDIOBOOK SET
~~$99.50~~ $75.00	~~$129.50~~ $97.00
ISBN: 978-1-61986-091-9	ISBN: 978-1-61986-092-6

☐ Check here if shipping address is same as billing.

Name

Billing Address

City   State   ZIP

Telephone   E-mail

Credit/Debit Card #: _____

Card ID # (last 3 or 4 digits): _____

Exp Date: _____/_____ Date (month/day/year): _____/_____/_____

Order Total *(CA and FL residents add sales tax)*: _____

To order online, go to: **www.GoldenAgeStories.com** or call toll-free **1-877-8GALAXY** or 1-323-466-7815

Then the Winchester fell and, stiff and hard, Johnny crashed down on top of it, his spurs making a small *chink-chink* before the stillness settled.

There were other men here. They did not show. The two dead ones lay with open eyes which did not see Mart ride away.

His next step was the Lawson jail and there, to his unspeakable relief, he found Gary safe, halfway through his breakfast.

Corby Tate, the marshal, looked wonderingly at Mart.

"Kincaid," he said, getting up from his overstuffed office chair, "I thought yuh was up there around Tumbleweed."

"How about letting Gary have a parole, Tate? I'll answer."

"Do yuh think I'd be fool enough to try to argue it out with *you* if the prisoner took it into his head to run away? Can't. Besides, the Federal marshal just put him in here for safekeepin' till he could get around to shippin' him up to Leadville for a trial."

"You know Gary never killed anybody," said Mart.

"Not only don't I know that, Kincaid, but I ain't even got the right to think about this case." He looked over Mart's shoulder. "Here's yore man. Harris, this is Kincaid, O'Neil's foster brother."

The US marshal shook Mart's hand. "Heard something of you, Kincaid."

"Glad to know yuh, Harris. What's happened here? I been away."

"Yeah, the youngster said you'd be down for him. But don't try any gunplay, Kincaid. It isn't that you couldn't win. But this

isn't anything for you to go to jail about, too. And whatever
I heard, I don't think you're ripe for the owl-hoot line of
business. All I know is that Jeb Barly came over and said he
had orders to hand yours truly a packet he'd been keeping in
his safe. And it was a letter from Leadville saying that Gar
Malone was correct in supposing that one Gary O'Neil had
been part of a gang that killed four miners in cold blood. So
that's all I knew."

"Letter say anything else?"

"Nope."

"Man named Tom Bellows ran the gang. I don't know what
kind a gent he was. But he snaked the kid into lookin' over
the setup, then Bellows and his own gang went in and did
the business. When the kid found out there'd been killin' he
wouldn't touch an ounce of the concentrate. I've knowed all
about this for more'n five years, Harris. The kid never did
another crooked thing in his life."

"Well, sorry I can't help more."

"Yes, yuh can," said Mart. "Malone heard about this from
some place and he must know either Bellows or one of the
gang. Oh, don't think Malone don't know plenty men on the
dodge. You help me locate Malone. If we find one of the real
killers, how about lettin' the kid go? After all, he never took
part in any of it."

Harris scratched his head. In this violent and untamed
land he was used to strange bargains.

"You seem to think Malone has become hard to find," he
offered.

"Yep."

"All here don't meet the eye, Kincaid."

"All right, I'll spill it. I worked for Malone because he blackmailed me with what he knew about O'Neil. I couldn't quit. For some reason, Malone broke his part of the bargain. Now it's my turn to find Malone and pull some of the same."

"Blackmail?"

"Prison. I haven't been his gun hand for five years without gettin' filled up to the eyes with his dirt. I got some mighty interestin' evidence on a lot of yore unsolved crimes, Harris. I didn't do 'em, but I know who did, and it's time justice got unblindfolded."

Harris was a small, neat man, not at all what one would consider a gunslinging officer. But he said, "Well, reckon I better oil up the artillery, Kincaid. You made yourself a bargain. Don't think Malone won't fight, though. You interested, Tate?"

"Nope," said Tate promptly. "Even if it was in my district, I'd think twice before I baited Gar Malone. He may be good and he may be bad with guns. I wouldn't know. But Kincaid wasn't the only lead investor he had on the payroll. And he left here three days ago with a pretty tough crew."

Harris smiled. "Don't blame you, Tate. Wait until I get some breakfast, Kincaid, and we'll ride."

Shortly before noon Mart and Harris burned sand for the Tumbleweed country. It irked Mart to have to slacken his pace so that Harris could stay with him, but he bemused himself with a promise of what would come when he found Malone. There was a plenty big score to pay for these five years.

And who had broken the truce? Not Kincaid.

They stopped and rested when the sun got too hot, and

they ate cold chuck. Harris would have stayed until the sun was well down, but Kincaid argued him into keeping on.

"Why," said Harris as they were in the saddle again, "do you think he'll be in the Tumbleweed country?"

"That was the order of business. And I was there. And he won't figger he's safe till he nails me. Let's use up some of this hossflesh, Harris."

It was late when they cautiously entered the headquarters of Hot Rock. Everything was quiet there—no lights, no sound from the bunkhouse. Mart walked gingerly into one building after another, then halted at the corral. There wasn't a single horse there.

Puzzled, he came back to Harris. "Something has happened here," he said. "If I ain't readin' this sign wrong, everybody pulled out of here today on a flat run."

Harris pushed his small hat back and rubbed his brow.

"Kincaid, I don't happen to be made out of whang leather and Tabasco sauce like you. Eighty-nine miles over this country is a power of travel. Let's sleep on it three, four hours and get out by moonrise. I'll kill myself yet on these rocks and cactuses."

Grudgingly, Mart led his horse toward the owner's shack, and Harris thankfully followed. But when he reached the door Mart stopped dead. Stale powder smoke had reached his nostrils—and something else.

He hastily tied his reins on the veranda rail and cat-footed inside. Harris heard his jinglebobs moving in the next room, then a lucifer flared and through the door Harris saw a terrible thing.

The bed which Mart had so recently used was blowed with six slugs and the mattress was soaked with dried blood. The empty brass was underfoot, but the body was gone.

Mart had hopes for a moment that Malone had come here and been killed. He lighted a lamp and inspected things more closely. Harris pointed to blood spots on the big white Navajo rug of the main room and they followed these.

The trail led down the steps and then two grooves appeared in the sand.

"Draggin' a dead'n," said Mart. "Them's his heels."

The twin furrows wound into the pines and ended on the edge of an irrigation ditch. Part of the bank had been moved, and the earth was dry from the day's sunlight.

"Must have happened early today," said Mart. "This ground's awful dry."

They found sticks and dug in the soft turf. In ten minutes they had Brazos' body in the pale flare of the lamp. The boy had been shot repeatedly in the face and chest.

"The poor kid!" sobbed Mart. "He never had a chance. Somebody must have—" He stood up. "Harris, I see it. The kid went to bed in my bunk after I left. Before daylight somebody came in and kilt him and dragged his body out here and buried it. They think he was me. They think I'm dead. The poor kid! Harris, Malone is really goin' to pay high for this one!"

They took Brazos into a bunkhouse, laid his body on a table and covered him with a blanket. Then, with no further complaints from Harris, they mounted once more.

CHAPTER EIGHT

Paid in Full

IT was Mart's intention to head for Tumbleweed a few miles out. Harris drew up and stared at the horizon. "There's a fire over there," he commented.

Mart looked at the dull red glow above the desert rim, and then at the stars. He brought down his quirt and started for the blaze.

"That's the SC headquarters!" he yelled over his shoulder. "And that's where we'll find Malone!"

They kited over the rough ground for six miles before they found a trail, then Mart let his worn bronc drop to a trot. Harris came up with him and they rode in silence, eyes on the flames ahead.

As they rimmed a gulch, they were squarely faced by the blaze, not a thousand yards away. They could see small figures dashing back and forth before the fire. Evidently the house had been fired first, for the barn was just beginning to go and a bunkhouse was about half burned.

A horse was screaming where someone was trying to get him out of a stall. Other stock was being led hurriedly to safety.

Mart came up to the small crowd which had abandoned attempts at fighting the conflagration and found himself next to Drake.

*As they rimmed a gulch, they were squarely faced
by the blaze, not a thousand yards away.*

"What happened?" Mart demanded.

"That Kincaid and his Malone gunners!" stormed Drake. "They rode in here and threw pitch-pine torches into the house and haystacks. Shot two men and got away. By the Eternal—"

Suddenly he grabbed for his gun, his face livid.

Mart had his wrist. Harris threw Drake back.

"Don't be a fool," said Harris, shoving his badge up where the flames glanced from it. "Kincaid was nowhere near this place. It must have been Malone in person."

Sally thrust through the press.

"I told them you didn't! I told them you didn't! Oh, Mart, I'm so glad you've come! Don't let Pa go after Malone. He'll get killed!"

Mart nodded to her briefly. "Which way did the crowd go, Drake?"

"South. By the eternal, Kincaid, I'm beginnin' to believe somebody told a lot of lies about you! Sally, and then me, and now this. I'll get some men—"

"Don't need men," said Mart. "Come on, Harris."

They took two fire-skittish horses, changed saddles, and by the light of the burning headquarters mounted and struck out.

The fire lighted the country a long way around and by its glare they read sign. Malone, if Malone it was, had traveled fast toward Tumbleweed, had cut back to the Hot Rock trail and had evidently headed straight for that ranch.

Mart swore when he saw it. Had they waited a few minutes even, they might have ambushed Malone in safety.

Harris several times had to call Mart back, and just before they reached the outskirts of the pine grove, lectured caution. Mart finally agreed and they dismounted and went forward on foot.

Mart was startled to hear singing far off. Evidently several riders, drunk, were returning at a leisurely pace from Tumbleweed. By the faint moonlight, Harris urged haste now where he had indicated caution. At a silent run they cut back of the bunkhouses and halted, seeing a lamp in the owner's shack.

Mart thrust Harris behind him. Stiff-legged, he went forward and silently came to the veranda. Through the open door he could see Gar Malone.

The man who had made Concha Basin a Hades was slumped over a freshly made fire, warming his hands around a glass of hot whiskey. He looked nervous and tired.

Mart stepped firmly on the porch and walked to the door.

"That you, Tom?" said Malone. "I been waitin'. Did yuh get it done?"

He took a drink, not yet having looked at the door. Mart stood there, leaning against the panel, thumbs hooked in his belt. He grunted an assent.

"Well, we still got the law with us. Boys all in town. You and . . . Thunderation!"

He said it as a groan and the whiskey glass fell from slacked fingers to tinkle and splash on the hearth.

"You got a gun," said Mart. "Go for it."

"You— I thought—"

"I ain't dead. Go for it!"

Malone shook his head wildly. He stood up, unbuttoned his coat and carefully hooked out his short gun from its spring holster and let it fall to the floor.

The fire popped and showered sparks on the hearth.

"By Tom, mebbe yuh mean Tom Bellows," said Mart.

Malone's pallor lightened and his eyes flashed for an instant. It was enough.

Mart turned to call Harris into the room. It was only a slight click which warned him. He doubled up and fell to the floor just as a gun flashed.

Malone had shucked a holdout Derringer from his sleeve. The second barrel flamed and a soft-nosed slug tore lightning through Mart's left shoulder.

His own guns were on their way out. Three fast explosions slammed from the window and Mart's gun flew from his right hand. He cross-drew as he rolled.

Boot Hill Smitty was there on the veranda, having a hard time getting far enough around for a fatal shot.

"Kill him!" screamed Malone. "Kill him, Tom!" He scrambled for his fallen short gun.

Suddenly Malone straightened up. Delayed he might have been, wounded he was. But Mart Kincaid knew where his shots went.

The first took Malone dead center and back. The second knocked him into a jackknife. The third kicked out the lamp.

Mart rolled wildly to avoid another shot from Smitty, and snapped one at the gun flame.

Boot Hill Smitty screamed. A shot racketed outside and Smitty, onetime Tom Bellows, fell writhing over the sill, shot in the chest by Mart, in the back by Harris.

The acrid smoke drifted bluely in the firelight. Smitty was coughing faintly, but from Malone came no sound.

Mart sat up and felt his shoulder with his bleeding hand.

"How is it?" said Harris, giving him a cigarette.

"Burns like blazes, but there's nothin' broke. Glad I had a good witness. Clear-cut case." He nodded toward Smitty. "He called himself Tom Bellows once. He might be able to talk."

Smitty had little time, and his dangerous eyes were dangerous no more. They were staring with terror. He didn't want to die.

Mart heard him say what Harris wanted to know, and saw Harris writing names of men and whereabouts down, nodding once and again, bribing Smitty with slugs of whiskey.

Then Mart passed out. . . .

Three days later Mart Kincaid got a wire from Lawson. He was sitting on the foreman's porch, for he'd had the owner's shack closed. His arm was in a sling and his guns hung over the back of his chair. He was smiling pleasantly at Sally as she swung down from her pinto, extending him the wire.

The Drakes had moved into Hot Rock and five new riders had replaced the old Malone crew. The sun of September was warm and soft through the pines.

"Read your telegram," said Sally. "Maybe that'll stop your frettin'."

Mart grinned at her, unfolded it, and read:

MART. DONE WHAT YOU SAID AND IT'S OKAY.
WHAT WITH LAWSUITS FOR OLD SCORES
MALONE ESTATE NOT WORTH SECONDHAND
SAGEBRUSH. EXECUTORS OKAY HOT ROCK
TO YOU TWENTY THOUSAND LOCK STOCK
AND BARREL. FOUND OUT MALONE GUNS ON
MALONE ORDERS STOLE THAT GIRL. YOU
BUTTED IN. THEY RID BACK TO SAY YOU'VE
SOLD OUT AND MALONE ACTED ACCORDIN.
SENT DESTRO UP TO KILL YOU BUT DESTRO
LOST NERVE AND CAME BACK TO SAY YOU
WERE GUN FOR DRAKE NOW. MALONE HAD ME
CABOOSED FOR REVENGE. WENT PERSONAL
WITH MAN NAMED SMITTY WHO TURNED UP
HERE TO KILL YOU AND YOU KNOW REST.
HARRIS TURNED ME LOOSE. TWO BELLOWS
GANG WERE HERE LOCAL AND GOT CAUGHT.
WAS SMITTY BELLOWS QUESTION MARK. MOM
SENDING YOU APPLE PIE BY STAGE. KEEP YORE
GUNS IN LEATHER AND DON'T DO NOTHING
I WOULDN'T. THANKS.
                        GARY O'NEIL

Someone came up onto the porch.

"Excuse me," said old man Drake. "I didn't see yuh were readin'."

"It's all right," said Mart. "Nothin' could spoil my plumb happiness."

"We got our temporary quarters rigged up here," said Drake, "and it's mighty fine of yuh. I'm sendin' a crew over to get things started and we should be out of yore hair being winter."

"Yuh ain't in anybody's hair," said Mart. "I figger yuh got more'n this comin' to yuh after the deal yuh picked up."

"Well, we can't stay here forever," said Drake. "By the way, I hope yuh come by the spread like yuh said."

"It's here," said Mart, giving him the telegram.

Drake read it and grinned. "Didn't know a gunhawk like you ate apple pie."

"Gunhawk?" said Mart. "Drake, yuh see before yuh the confounded most peaceful citizen in Concha Basin. I'm settin' back to enjoy my five years' pay right here on Hot Rock and, by crickets, I earned every last cent of this and twenty spreads like it. Malone owed me for five years of perdition and I bet it don't help his temper none, hoppin' around down there on them red-hot coals, to know that he come close to puttin' me in heaven for the rest of my days."

Drake nodded. "Then yuh'll stay with us?"

"You bet. Yuh couldn't drive me away from Hot Rock. I got the most rooted feet yuh ever saw on a man. Besides, I got to wait four or five years for my special project to come off."

"What's that?" said Drake.

Mart grinned. Sally in some confusion stamped down the steps and led her pinto off to the corral.

But she wasn't mad.

Blood on His Spurs

CHAPTER ONE

War in His Whiskers

IRON JAW BATES took one hard look at the interloper and his quirt popped like a pistol shot. The startled roan went catapulting down the shale slide, across the wash, up the bank and sawed wind on the trail of the enemy. Belly almost touching the prickly pear, the black gelding ahead appeared to be leaving the country. His tall rider did not look back but pumped fury into the mount.

With mesquite whipping his tattered batwings, utterly careless of holes, rocks and gullies, Iron Jaw was on his way to get his man. And the only trouble with the chase was that Iron Jaw, old enough himself, was riding a horse past prime, paying penalty for ease in his declining years.

It would take wit, not speed, to cut down Larry McClean.

Ahead was a castle of rock, based with tumbles of giant stone. If Iron Jaw saw the other's course aright, it would be possible to cut short on this curve and, by being merciless with quirt and spur, reach directly Rosarita Canyon and block the way with lead.

Oblivious of pursuit, Larry McClean rode hard and fast. Oblivious of boundaries, he did not see that he was far inside another man's range.

Iron Jaw clove hot New Mexico air, risked his aging limbs

in a final leap across a gully and drew up, guns flashing in the sunlight squarely in front of his enemy.

"Stand him up, McClean!"

Larry McClean, fifty and wise with years, already heard buzzards' wings as he brought the black gelding to a halt. Carefully he kept his hands away from guns. He was a cold, hard man and he could be prudent.

"What the heck you doin'?" bellowed Iron Jaw. "Next Rocking Chair man crossed that line, I said I'd bury. Now I'm going to bury the boss. If you got any touching appeals, Larry McClean, make 'em, because the world ain't goin' to be gladdened by yore presence no more."

McClean looked down the trail toward the gaping mouth of the Rosarita Canyon and then for the first time seemed to see the range where he had arrived. In plain sight, two thousand yards south, there among the poplars, was the main ranch house of Iron Jaw's Spread Eagle.

"Git down!" ordered Iron Jaw. "Can't shoot a man when his horse is champin' and prancin'."

"Must be gettin' old," said McClean. "Down on the Panhandle you'd never have admitted failin' eyesight. But that was thirty years back. You really goin' to shoot?"

"And what's the matter with that? My stock is gone, my men has quit—them that's still alive. And the Rocking Chair looks fat enough to account for it. I told you 'No trespassin'' and that didn't mean excursions on my grass. Get down and be decent about it."

"I'll get down and be decent," said McClean, "but you're

lettin' a hell of a good chance go sailin' off. See that trail? I followed it two hours from a warm brandin' fire and eight mismatched calves and cows. If you're interested, we'll postpone the 'dobe wallin' and get some rustlers."

"I don't see no trail."

"You couldn't see a rattler in yore oatmeal!" said Larry McClean. "You want to know what them calves was branded with?"

"No."

"Okay, to heck with it."

"Well," snarled Iron Jaw, "out with it!"

"The Spread Eagle," said McClean, tauntingly.

Iron Jaw's fists shook around his gun butts. "You inferrin'—?"

"Iron Jaw, I got forty-one riders and a hundred square miles of range filled with cows that make your best steer look like an ad for the before—"

"I ain't got no steers. And no wonder yore range is full. Stop yappin' and start dismountin'. Dang that horse of yourn!"

"Sheriff came out and said Cotton Vasquez was up here with six owl-hoots and that border traffic had been heavy on Spread Eagle and Rocking Chair beef. Here!" McClean took out a paper and shoved it at Iron Jaw. The old man didn't see the contempt in McClean's eyes.

The old man turned it around doubtfully. He was too stubborn to buy specs and too proud to admit his eyes were failing. The writing was a shivering blur, but he gritted his teeth and made out the scrawl.

Iron Jaw,

Keep an eye peeled for strangers. If you can come in, I got eighteen head of your cattle corralled that we got off a bunch bein' bordered. Cotton Vasquez's head *vaquero* got drunk in town last night and we buried him this morning. Cotton's got two owl-hoots with him and four dark ones from the other side. Keep close to home and send in quick if trouble starts.

George

Iron Jaw wadded the paper up and threw it down. He shoved his guns back in their holsters and scowled darkly at McClean.

"You probably hired him," grumbled Iron Jaw. "How come it's all my stock and none of yourn?"

"The man wants to see us fight," said McClean.

"He wouldn't have to look hard," said Iron Jaw.

The two men glowered at each other. The animosity was deep and burned in with twenty years of brooding. Iron Jaw, stubborn and cantankerous, felt he had real reasons to hate his onetime saddlemate. After that fight down in the Panhandle, they'd ceased to be friends. McClean had always been smarter, cooler, better off than Iron Jaw. That's why the girl had leaned toward him.

After they'd shot it out that night long ago, McClean had taken her away. For twenty years, more or less, Iron Jaw had tried to forget it. And then, by accident it seemed, McClean had cut in and been made ramrod of the Rocking Chair by the big Eastern syndicate. Suddenly, unbeknownst to either until three weeks ago, they had become neighbors.

Bad blood such as theirs took more sun and years than this to purify.

McClean looked at the empty range around him. There were a few wild horses in a nearby holding fence. That was all. He looked back at Iron Jaw, feigning a concern, hiding amusement.

"They really got you cleaned out?"

"They or you did. I only had fifteen hundred head but that was choice enough. I could have weathered it. And now you appear—"

"If I'm not going to be shot this afternoon, I'd better be getting home. Where's that canyon lead, Iron Jaw?"

"To heck and gone up in the hills. There's forty branches of it, five of them with rivers in 'em that disappear. Might as well look around," he added sarcastically. "You'll be owner of this before many moons pass."

McClean wheeled the black roan, and bits of foam collected on his buff riding pants. He carefully brushed his knee, looking absently at the empty range. He looked back at Iron Jaw.

"All you got is them horses?" said McClean.

"They'll do," said Iron Jaw. Then, suddenly, "Where's Mary?"

A shadow passed over McClean's lean face. "She's been dead these past ten years, Iron Jaw."

Silently he reined around and let the roan pick his way over the back trail.

CHAPTER TWO

Iron Jaw Hires an Iron Rider

A FTER a while Iron Jaw found out where he was sitting and looked about. McClean was a speck in the clear distance; the mountains just to the north were aloof and cool; the ranch house, empty of everyone but Sam Wong, the Chinese cook, seemed to be a strange and unfamiliar place to him.

He rode silently to the door and stiffly dismounted. He shook off the black cloud of tragedy and brought the corral into focus. He stopped, startled. The gate was open and forty head of stock were gone!

Iron Jaw needed that stock. The government would buy his saddlers at enough to weather him through, rustlers or no rustlers. And if forty of his two hundred head—

"Sam!" he bellowed. "Sam Wong! Sam, who the hell opened that gate?"

Iron Jaw almost fell across the Kid who sat on the stone step of the ranch house.

"I did," said the youngster, simply.

Iron Jaw looked hard at him. There was something vaguely haunting about the Kid's face. But eyesight bad or good, Iron Jaw suddenly realized he had not seen him before.

The Kid was very tall, young and sunburned. He was

wearing the signs of hard riding but he carried no gun and his clothes were neat. He was the kind of a man who would shave every morning, decided Iron Jaw. Probably a tenderfoot.

"I suppose," said Iron Jaw dangerously, "that you had good reason for it?"

"I did," said the Kid.

"'I did'!" mimicked Iron Jaw. "That all you can say?"

"No, sir. I can add that the stud in there dang near killed himself on the bars. I took them out into the holding corral where he could run it off."

Iron Jaw glared toward the holding corral. As he brought it into focus it came to him that the Kid was right. About two hundred head were in there, the right number.

"And how come you took this on yourself?"

The Kid built himself a careful smoke. "I guess I figured you needed a horse wrangler. And if you didn't need a horse wrangler, then maybe a buckaroo."

"What'd you say yore name was?"

"Didn't say, boss. But 'the Kid' will serve."

Iron Jaw suddenly remembered the note. He looked at this tall rider. No gun. No sign of drinking. Just like any other drifter, except he kept himself better.

"How do I know you can break sticks, much less horses?" demanded Iron Jaw.

The Kid took a final puff on his smoke, ground it out in the sand of the walk, picked up a sixty-foot rawhide riata and started to walk toward the holding corral.

"Hold up there," said Iron Jaw. "Ain't you got no horse of your own?"

"Nope," said the Kid.

But Iron Jaw saw the saddle that had been dragged many a weary mile. It was sitting on the porch, a rimfire, very plain, very old. It had two bullet holes through the right skirt. The apple horn had a lead streak on it. The marks might be new, they might be old. Who could tell?

Hastily Iron Jaw picked up the saddle and bridle and, boosting them up on the old roan, led out after the Kid.

Iron Jaw was so jumpy that when he heard soft footfalls behind him he jumped and half drew. But it only frightened Sam Wong.

The cook, with a celestial yellow moon for a face, liked to watch bucking horses, liked an occasional quiet pipe, liked to sing terrible Chinese songs and would not be separated from Iron Jaw whom he considered a sort of green-eyed devil, a personal god of forked-lightning speech and a gross inability to be a tenth as cruel as he sounded.

Sam Wong grinned and took a seat on the top rail.

"Him prenty loung," said Sam Wong.

The Kid had singled out a bay that was all saddle scars. He was a renegade that somebody had kept as a bucking horse. Iron Jaw had hopes that the government would overlook the matter and consider the saddle scars a token of being broken. Actually Wall Eye was the most dangerous horse in the big corral.

The Kid neatly forefooted him, snubbed him into the makeshift chute, saddled him and prepared to ride.

Sam Wong obligingly threw the gate. Wall Eye was wise. He walked out calm as a kitten, suddenly reared to knock his rider off against the bar, turned and would have jammed a leg against a post and then would have rolled. But when the dust cleared the Kid was up there, hat going, yelling and digging spur.

Wall Eye went wild. He sunfished and screamed and tried to tear the saddle with his teeth. He went down but when he came up the Kid was still riding.

Dust grew. The maddened horse lunged into everything he could find and finally somersaulted when he missed the gate. He came up. The Kid was in the saddle.

For twelve minutes the outlaw tried his tricks and went crazy when they failed. And then, spent and shuddering, Wall Eye stood in the center of the corral, legs apart, head down. Sam Wong was in ecstasy.

The Kid dismounted and patted the ex-bucker's neck. He fumbled in his pockets for sugar, found none and began to uncinch.

"Good lide! Good lide!" screamed Sam Wong.

"Shut up, you caterwauling freak!" snarled Iron Jaw.

"Good lide!" yelled Sam Wong. "You catch biscuits and Flench flied potatoes tonight. Good lide!"

"I ain't hired him," said Iron Jaw.

"You more big fool. You catchee hell tly bleak two horses muchee ress two hundred. Good lide. Boss hire. Him good man."

"Guess you don't have much to say," said the Kid with a grin to Iron Jaw.

Iron Jaw tried to frown. He had been so impressed with

the ride he was ashamed of himself. There was a time when he could have ridden like that.

Still, that note . . . He looked at the Kid's face. He looked again and something made it hard for him to swallow. He liked this youngster even if he didn't have any right.

"I got to break all two hundred in three weeks," said Iron Jaw. "Some are half-gentled. Some are plumb wild. The government wants 'em and if I don't sell, there won't be any Spread Eagle. It would normally take a full crew two months. Can you do it?"

The Kid built himself a smoke, leaning against the corral posts. "Yep," he said.

And all that night Iron Jaw tossed around kicking himself for being a fool. What did he know of this Kid? One of Cotton's gang. Couldn't be anything else. And what a smart move, to come in here, break the herd into a semblance of riding horses and then pull out with the lot of them.

And when he could manage to forget the Kid he would remember what a jackass he had made of himself that day before McClean and would kick himself for not shooting on sight. Talk, talk, talk. That was the trouble with him. When he was young he'd acted fast and talked afterwards.

Well, he wasn't young now. And he had little ahead of him. He had tried to patch up his life where it had broken. He had furiously doped himself with ambition to be a cattle king. A month ago he had been fairly well off. Now he was just another rancher, nearly broke, harnessed by debts and few enough prospects even if he did manage to sell those horses.

Horses and cattle. Poor enough substitutes for a home and a family. But Larry McClean had broken all that. And hadn't Larry McClean come just before the Spread Eagle itself was broken? Before morning he fell into a tortured sleep wherein he shot it out again with McClean only to find he had killed the Kid by mistake. And Sam Wong was accusing him of murder.

But it wasn't murder. Sam Wong was accusing him of sleeping an hour after sunup.

"Kid bleakee six horses alleady!" reproved Sam. "Sun prenty catchee you. Blekfas' in stove. Me go back and cheer. No man can bleak horses if nobody yell 'Good lide!'"

Iron Jaw got out of his sack and into his clothes, groaning with rheumatism. He looked at his stubbled face in the cracked mirror and saw suddenly how old and haggard he was. Too many bucking broncs, too many years on the hard ground. Too much frostbite and too many dry camps. Hell of a chance he had to go on living. They wouldn't take him in as a cook's helper on the meanest spread in the Southwest.

He clenched his jaw with resolve. This was his last battle. He had to be man enough to fight it, for if he lost it, he was gone for keeps.

Outside, the clear New Mexico air sparkled in the morning sunlight. A haze of golden dust glittered above the corral and under it men's legs and horses' legs threshed. The ranch was filled with the bawl of outraged mounts and the crack and slap of leather.

It mystified him that there seemed to be too many men

present. And as soon as he had eaten his fried cornmeal and sowbelly he got down to the corral to find out who.

The Kid had just smashed the surly temper of a big bay into a beaten pulp and was resaddling. But he had one more helper than Sam Wong.

Apologetically, Dirty Watson came up out of the dust and said, "Howdy, Iron Jaw."

"What the heck are you doing back here?" roared Iron Jaw.

"Sure, I knowed I quit. I was scared of bullets then," whined Dirty. "They'd nicked Fred and kilt Pete Colorado. But I come back."

He wanted it to be a brave and loyal gesture but Iron Jaw knew. A man could be scared of bullets when he had a belly full of grub and a credit on the payroll. But after six days of constant drinking in Six-gun's rotgut palaces, with his cash run out and no job offered even to clean spittoons, he got more scared of starvation than he had been of the bullets. You can duck lead.

"You miserable misfortune!" said Iron Jaw. "What I need is a horse breaker and you turn up! I got a notion—"

"Oh, you'll hire me," said Dirty with underdog assurance. "The Kid can't cut 'em out, hold 'em, saddle 'em, ride 'em and tally all day, and fight rustlers all night."

"Tell Sam Wong to feed you and get back to work. I'll sweat that whiskey out of yore filthy hide."

"I alleady feed," announced Sam Wong. "Ret 'er bluck!"

The Kid had a quiet one and the ride was no more than a tour of the corral. All these horses had been halter broke, snubbed and blanketed. On most of them only a final ride was missing. The Kid looked tall and clean in the saddle and the old man felt something like a lump in his throat again.

If he could have had a son like that!

"Hiya, Iron Jaw!" grinned the Kid as he finished the ride. "A hundred and ninety-three to go." He whacked off a twist of mane to mark the horse and let Dirty lead him away and resaddle.

The Kid permitted himself a breather. His lean face was flushed with repeated victories and his blond hair was damp with sweat. He built a smoke, leaning against the corral. "My leather ain't goin' to stand all the beatin' it'll get. I guess you got a buckin' saddle."

"I got a Californy I won in a stud game. It'll do. Kid . . ."

"Well?"

"I ain't asked you what I should put down on the payroll."

"I'll sign it with a big *X* anyhow," said the Kid. "So you think one up."

"I don't like it too well, Kid. I . . . well, I appreciate what yore doin' for me here and I'll pay you even if it's in land, though that ain't worth nothin'. If you can make it, I'll sell these horses and you got five dollars a head and a steady winter job. But . . ."

"Well, dang it! I been rustled blind. Fifteen hundred head has went up Rosarita Canyon. Two hundred fine horses ain't goin' to follow if I can help it."

"Iron Jaw, if I was a hoss thief, do you think I'd be killin' myself breakin' these plugs? Come on off, man. What's my name is my business. What I can do is yore business. And

I'm doin' what I can do. You make your nine–ten thousand on these fuzz-tails. Let me make my one thousand and keep my job. I ain't asked for yore right name."

Iron Jaw flushed. And then he couldn't get mad. The Kid was grinning, and the grin was infectious. Even Dirty Watson had cheer and enthusiasm around here.

"You made yore place and yore holdin' it," said Iron Jaw. And then because he hated to be thought easy and good-natured, he suddenly changed the subject. "You ain't packin' artillery. Got any?"

"Nope."

Iron Jaw removed his own belt and handed it over. He was wearing his spare. "We been known to have trouble around here."

"Who from?" said the Kid, eyeing the weapon with distrust.

"The Rocking Chair. Larry McClean has tooken over. Since he come there's been nothin' but trouble on this place. It's a big Eastern outfit and . . . What's the matter?"

The Kid was not smiling. He looked kind of white. "Nothin'."

"Well, I'd hate to think you didn't like a fight. If them Rocking Chair rannies show up here or if McClean comes on the place, you better shoot first and discourse later. It'll keep you in better health."

The Kid didn't say anything. He wasn't smiling. He hung the gun and belt over the top bar of the gate and went back to mount a dun that showed signs of disliking all mankind in general and the Kid in particular.

CHAPTER THREE

Spurs Roll on the Spread Eagle

FOR three weeks they fought horses and marked manes and the bright New Mexico days were full of yells and dust and the smell of hot leather until at last they were coming out to the end of the horse herd.

It had been murderous work and the Kid was tired. He dragged an aching body from an all-too-brief night of corpse-tired sleep and mounted up to show more horses who was boss. Sam Wong put mustang liniment on his bruises and laughed at his jokes and Dirty Watson mended girths and hazed wild ones and was even heard to sing.

The Kid's spirit was everywhere in the ranch where only gloom had reigned so long. His high, *"Yi-yi-yi!"* as he beat a bronco's ears echoed far on the range. Iron Jaw began to forget the fifteen hundred head of rustled cows.

The government buyer was on his way and soon there'd be a little cash left from paid debts and he and the Kid could go down to Texas and bring up a few hundred shorthorns to feast on Spread Eagle grass. Maybe he'd save a stake for his old age after all.

He piled up his books in his scrubby little office and went down toward the corral.

"Good lide!" yelled the cheering section as he had ten times a day for the past three weeks.

Iron Jaw climbed a rail, withdrew a toothpick and yelled at the Kid. Dirty Watson took over the staggering and dismayed bronc. The Kid patted the lathered neck of the gelding.

"Never mind," said the Kid. "In a few weeks some soldier will be trying that and you can get even—plenty! Hi, Iron Jaw!"

"Hi, yourself," said Iron Jaw, unable to keep from smiling. The Kid looked leaner and harder for his punishing weeks of work. And as Iron Jaw looked at him, he had again that haunting sensation that he had seen him somewhere before. "I'm taking Sam Wong into town for grub, Kid. We got just about enough to feed a sick canary. Besides, that buyer might be in Six-gun right now wondering how to find his way onto the Spread Eagle." He grinned in anticipation.

"Gone long?" said the Kid.

"Tomorrow morning back sure. We'll be driving eighteen head the sheriff is holding for me out of a bunch that McClean lost when he bordered the last herd. Keep yore eye peeled and look after these hosses. They're all that stands between me and starvation." He settled his hat, got down and motioned for Sam Wong to follow.

"Iron Jaw," said the Kid, hesitating. There was a scared look in his eyes.

"Yeah?"

"You . . . er . . . going to see the sheriff?"

"Sure. How the heck— Oh. I savvy." He frowned.

The Kid rubbed his shoulders like he was cold. "It ain't quite as bad as you think, Iron Jaw. But I'd shore appreciate it if you wouldn't mention me."

"All right. All right," said Iron Jaw, ruffled and unhappy. "Take care of things, Dirty."

He walked stiffly to the south corral and cut out the chuck wagon team. Sam Wong was torn between town and more bucking shows. He was saddened by the thought that no further entertainment would be forthcoming in the corral for a while. And then, as the moon-faced celestial harnessed up he remembered that the Kid would be staying on and he brightened into a caterwaul that he was shortly forced to explain to Iron Jaw as a song about two soldiers far from home who had lost their mother.

Iron Jaw didn't allow any more singing. Alert on the box he rolled the wagon along the trail to Six-gun. His Winchester was handy and his eyes were sharp. He could see pretty well from a hundred yards on out. It was just up close stuff that worried him. And he could see fine enough to plug Rocking Chair people at any range.

But no targets bowed forth and he made an uneventful trip.

There were delays in Six-gun that evening. The buyer wasn't there but a letter said he was due the following Saturday, three days off. Then there was the matter of the store bill which Jake Simmons was not willing to regard as slight. And the sheriff was long-winded about rustlers and very impatient at Iron Jaw's efforts to point out that trouble and McClean had come together. There were delays.

It was ten o'clock high before he got Sam Wong started on the wagon while he hazed eighteen head out in front from the back of his gentle roan.

A curious impatience to get home was gripping him. Something seemed to say, each time a steer broke free or gave trouble, "That's another vital minute you've lost, Iron Jaw."

With his rope end he made the cattle shuffle into a ragged gallop and then had to stop and re-form them hurriedly as they scattered far.

Sam Wong got lost somewhere in the plains behind as noon turned into two o'clock. Iron Jaw was in a white lather to get home and he ached to get to the boundaries of the Spread Eagle where he could turn the cattle loose on familiar ground and then high-tail it for the ranch.

When at last he was free he laid on with his quirt and, rheumatism or no rheumatism, burned miles to headquarters. He came streaking down an arroyo and out on a bench close by the Rosarita Canyon and with a final slash at the offended roan, poured down the slope toward the ranch house.

Before he was within half a mile he could feel the deserted quiet in the place. At a quarter of a mile, streaking belly to bluegrass, he saw the empty corrals. Skidding to a dusty whirlwind, he flung himself from the saddle, dragging Winchester from boot, and rushed into the ranch house. There was no one there.

He sprinted to the bunkhouse and battered back the door. The place was empty. He stood irresolute before the gaping gate of the breaking corral and listened. Only the quiet sigh of New Mexico wind sounded in the day. A gunnysack flapped idly from a broken window in the office. A tumbleweed softly jarred its way across the yard.

Iron Jaw stood still. He was holding on hard. He had held

on hard for a long, long time and it seemed that there in the next instant something inside him would break. A whimper reached him. He whirled and found himself staring at a very filthy Dirty Watson who had climbed out from under the wagon shed.

Iron Jaw waited, braced.

Dirty shuffled to him, the guts scared clean out of him.

"They come about eight or nine. There was fifty of 'em. I couldn't have stopped them. Nobody could have. I was in the cookhouse washing up and I couldn't do a thing. Don't hit me, Iron Jaw. There's things more'n a man can do."

Iron Jaw waited.

Dirty wiped his nose on his sleeve and sniveled. "I woulda been killed if they'd seen me. I dived out of the cookhouse and under the wagon shed and I been keepin' close all day. I tell you there was fifty of 'em and they all had masks and guns.

"They shot the lock off the corral gate. Didn't even stop to lift the wire. And they run out the twenty head there. And they stampeded the lot out into the pasture where we had the rest and they went out of sight like the ground had opened. Don't hit me!"

Iron Jaw stood waiting.

"Last night that black stud knocked off the top bar and made a break. Come daylight the Kid saddled up and went looking for him down to the south somewhere. The tracks was plain.

"Eight or nine, while I was washing up in the cookhouse, these thirty or forty gents came down on the place and cleaned it out."

Iron Jaw asked his question then. "Was the Kid one of them?"

Dirty gaped. He hadn't thought of it. But now that he did, it looked pat. He hadn't seen a single face to remember. And he hadn't looked for the Kid. His eyes sought the ground.

A bitter, brutal fury was taking hold of old Iron Jaw. He hefted the Winchester. His eyes raked the buildings and came to rest on the open bunkhouse door. He went back to the bunkhouse.

The Kid's small war sack was still on his bunk. The Kid's sougan was spread out neatly under it. Iron Jaw grabbed the elkskin bag and began to maul the contents out.

A set of silver spurs came to light. Then a small gun, lady's size. A pair of boots that must have cost eighty dollars was followed by three neat linen shirts, some underwear and socks, and finally a smaller kit which contained shaving gear and a packet of papers. The last were avidly seized and in a moment Iron Jaw was turning into a bomb.

The first letter was neatly written and addressed to a banking firm in New York. It was many months old.

> Gentlemen:
>   This will introduce my son, to whom you will please advance the sum of one hundred dollars on the first of every month. On no occasion shall this amount be increased. Please bill Tate and Bradshaw of Chicago.
>   Thanking you for past favors,
>   I remain,
>   Laurence McClean

"His kid," whispered Iron Jaw. "His kid! He sent his kid over to break the horses."

There were other letters addressed to other people but Iron Jaw did not read them. There were photographs and he would have thrown them all away, but one, falling gently to the floor, smiled up at him.

It was Mary. And she smiled at him. Smiled at him across twenty empty years.

CHAPTER FOUR

Rough on the Rocking Chair

FOR an instant something in Iron Jaw sought to break. And then, with a roar of fury, he scattered the letters wide and raced to the door.

The roan had breathed and Iron Jaw mounted so savagely that the old horse reared in fright. Iron Jaw's spurs dug deep and the roan sprang out on the trail, hoofs thundering, mane and tail flying, heading for the Rocking Chair.

Iron Jaw rode hard, low in the saddle, Winchester on his pommel, spurs raking at every sign of unwillingness in the roan. He covered eight miles at quarter horse speed and would have gone straight in. But he saw his game instead.

A black gelding was riding fence and Larry McClean, alone, stopped in midsurvey of the bedding ground to look curiously at the wild figure which was racing toward him.

Larry McClean saw death and he did the only thing a wise man could do. He unbuckled his gun belt and dropped holsters to earth. He plucked the Winchester from its scabbard and tossed it down. Hands at shoulder height then, he waited for Iron Jaw to quiet the maddened roan.

In a frustrated fury, Iron Jaw bellowed, "You sneaking coyote! Pick up those guns! This is the finish fight. This is the finish I should have given you twenty years ago. I wasn't hit hard then. I could have shot you as you walked away.

*Larry McClean saw death and he did the only thing
a wise man could do. He unbuckled his gun belt
and dropped holsters to earth.*

But I thought of her and she loved you. She's dead now. Pick up those guns or I'll kill you as you set!"

Larry held his peace and kept his hands raised under the menace of the Winchester. He had just come from his number four line camp and he was going to number five. He was a long way from help both directions.

"You stole my remounts. You sent your kid to fool me—"

"My kid?" said Larry McClean, eyes wide. "You mean Race?"

"You sent your kid and you got my horses. Him and your riders come down on my spread this morning."

"Wait a minute!" snapped McClean. "Either you're loco or I am. Race is near three thousand miles from here. What's he doing on your spread?"

This jarred Iron Jaw. Not the words. The manner. Here was the Kid's old man getting mad clean through at the Kid.

"Talk it straight!" roared Iron Jaw. "You know—"

"All I know is that I sent Race east five months ago. I haven't heard a word from my people in New York about him. He never cared how we got along but just yesterday I wired to find out. You seen Race. Here? In New Mexico?"

"You know damned well . . ." but Iron Jaw was getting feeble about it. "Yes, here in New Mexico. On the Spread Eagle to be exact for the past month. Wait . . . wait. You didn't know . . . ?"

"Tall. Looks like his mother. You sure it was Race?"

"Looks . . . looks like Mary." Iron Jaw was losing his fire. He knew now why that boy's face had haunted him. Mary's boy.

"I sent him east to break his stubborn ways," said McClean.

"He swore he wouldn't go. He said he'd make his own way and that I didn't own him. He doesn't like what's expected of my son. Too friendly, too . . . too common. He's never taken orders from me."

"Wait, wait. Wait!" cried Iron Jaw. "Oh, my gosh! Mary's boy. He wouldn't steal. He must have seen the raid. If it really is Vasquez. Larry—the Kid is up in them hills someplace trailing a crowd that would roast him alive on sight. Maybe they've got him now! Kill me for a fool, Larry. But pick up those guns and ride!"

The roan had a large heart. He needed it in that headlong sprint back to a spur of the Rosarita Canyon. The black gelding, fresh as he was, could not spurn turf and cactus and plain fast enough to breast the madly driven roan.

They leaped gullies and scrambled up shale. They plunged over ledges and through a river. Rabbits and deer started up insanely from the rush of hooves.

In an hour of cannonball flight they came to the main canyon and there, mounts plunging crazy-eyed, they swung down, two old saddlemates on a trail, to examine the tracks of a horse herd with one shod mount following after.

They looked, strained, trying to hear what they dreaded up the canyon. And then they mounted again and, spurs deep, skimmed over the plain trail, reaching ever higher into the Dutchman Range.

It was nearly sunset when they heard the firing. It had the sound of something which had not just begun. That one gun answered many put frenzy into them but heartened them as well.

Skidding wide on turns, reckless of the boulders which strewed the ancient riverbed, they mounted up from gravel and burst, foam-flecked and yelling, into a meadow where the river had run wide.

Two hundred head were pawing and churning in terror against a pole fence which barred the far exit to the meadow. A stream roared between high banks of grass and the shots were sharp against its rolling strength.

The Kid was holed up behind a V of rocks and his mount was kicking out his life on the flat below him. The high, shrill scream of a ricochet went out from the barricade and the Kid shot twice, quickly, seeing the exposure of his own people.

The men across the stream were behind a copse of aspen. They had been dismounted when the Kid had struck and their horses were rearing, still saddled among the herd.

A rifle began to chop at Iron Jaw as fast as Cotton Vasquez could lever. Iron Jaw went down. He dived headlong into the stream, rolled in the fury of the current and then, spitting water and fury, charged the copse.

The black gelding was across in a single leap. Larry McClean's six-gun was blazing as hot as it had at Gettysburg. McClean went through, reared, and let his mount strike down as he came hurtling back.

Cotton Vasquez was howling above the shots and the roaring stream. Two of his men were down. A third staggered in a circle of agony, gripping his belly.

Two guns blazed straight into Iron Jaw's face. He dodged away from a seared cheek, sprang up on a log and felt his Winchester butt crush soggily into a skull. His shirt twitched and the powder scorched his ribs. The face was a blur and the Winchester was shattered.

Iron Jaw hurled himself at his target for want of lead. He was conscious of many churning men on every side and then he hit Cotton Vasquez dead center and carried him down.

Vasquez had a short gun and it caught in the holster. Vasquez was a blur of dust and blood and Spanish insanity. But the gun stayed caught and Iron Jaw's fists pounded home. For an instant Vasquez relaxed and would have doubled and sprung free. But the caught gun, still held hard by the holster, had Iron Jaw's finger through the trigger. The gun leaped out. Iron Jaw had it and jabbed down against the glitter of a knife. The gun went off five times and then there was a curious stillness in the meadow.

Iron Jaw rose to fight and found dead men. He had killed two he knew and saw now from the ornaments on the dead man's clothing that he had gotten Vasquez. Larry McClean was sitting shakily on the black gelding looking at the torn grass and broken shrubs. He saw that Iron Jaw was alive, and dismounted.

They went over the dead and the Kid limped down, holding a hand to his thigh where a slug had nicked him. Iron Jaw was puzzled. "There was two dead and one down. But who got the pair behind that log? I was here with Vasquez and you shot—"

"You did," said the Kid. "Wonderful shooting. They had Dad dead center from cover until you opened up with the short gun."

98

"I did?" Iron Jaw looked at the weapon in his hand. It was very blurry. But there were seven dead men in this meadow.

"Well, dang my eyes," said Iron Jaw. "I ain't so blind—Kid, yore hit!"

"Nicked but it's bleedin' some. They had a bottle, and some whiskey on it would be welcome."

"Hello, Race," said McClean, frostily.

"Hello, Dad," said the Kid. "I guess they just couldn't stand to a cavalry charge. I thought I was done for until I heard Iron Jaw's yell. They were mighty low on ammunition but not low enough to pass me up when the sun went down."

"You didn't go east," said McClean coldly. "You'd heard from your mother about Iron Jaw. And you worked your way like some common saddle tramp and took a job with my enemy, a job far, far below your proper station."

"Now, Larry," said Iron Jaw. "This ain't no time nor place to be a parent. This gent is worth any thirty punchers. He's the most uncommon common man I ever met in my life!"

"You don't understand, Iron Jaw. He was set on throwing his life away on range country. No education, no prospects—"

"What the heck are you talking about?" exploded Iron Jaw, looking up from his work at applying a whiskey compress to the wound. "You and me never had no education beyond the third grade and we made out. If you mean he was drinkin' and hellin'—"

"I wasn't!" said the Kid. "All I wanted was a chance to start on my own. What kind of a guy would stay on his father's rep and money all his life? What did I want with inheritance when I had my own two hands?" He looked stubbornly at his father. "I won't go back. I'm my own man."

"See?" said Iron Jaw to McClean. "Mary's boy." He smiled in triumph.

"Y'see," said Iron Jaw, "me and the Kid are goin' down to Texas and come up with some shorthorns when we deliver these here hosses. And when they're fat and sassy on Spread Eagle grass, why we'll go out and buy some more.

"You better watch out on that Rocking Chair, Larry. Me and the Kid over on the Spread Eagle are liable to wind up owning you lock, stock and tin cans."

"You and me?" said the Kid, puzzled, scared to hope he could keep his job.

"Shore," said Iron Jaw, gleefully grinning sideways at Larry McClean. "Yore a full-time, fifty-fifty, straight-up, registered and recognized partner of the Spread Eagle, Kid. And you can stop dodging sheriffs that might tell yore pop where you was. But daylight's burning. Can you ride, Kid?"

"Iron Jaw," said Mary's kid, "with you to take 'em right and me to take 'em left, I reckon I could ride straight through hellfire and come out grinnin' on t'other side. Give us a neighborly hand with these hosses, Mr. McClean. Me and my partner has got a long ways to go."

Story Preview

Story Preview

NOW that you've just ventured through some of the captivating tales in the Stories from the Golden Age collection by L. Ron Hubbard, turn the page and enjoy a preview of *King of the Gunmen*. Join gunfighter Kit Gordon, also known as "Suicide," "Smoke" or "Sudden Death," who pairs with a lawman to make one of the West's most unlikely duos. Caught between the feuding sheepherders and cattle ranchers of Yancy County, Arizona, Kit must choose to either run for his life or reveal he's a wanted fugitive and square off with one of the region's most vicious tyrants.

King of the Gunmen

THE outlook of Kit Gordon was as bleak as the tawny desert which writhed in the heat below his cliff. Never in his thirty-one years had he sunk so far or faced death in such a variety of ways.

And that was saying a great deal, as men had variously dubbed the lean gunslinger "Suicide," "Smoke" and "Sudden Death." From the Missouri to the Pacific, tales were told about the branding fires of the things Kit Gordon was supposed to have done—and sometimes he had done them and always, even if he had not, he was capable of the feats.

Few men could honestly swear that they had met him but his general appearance was very well known. He stood six feet one, hardly thick enough through the waist to cast a shadow were it not for his double guns, swelling out to broad and heavy shoulders which bore up a well-shaped head from which any man, no matter how blind, could have judged his quick intelligence.

His one compelling feature was his eyes. They were changeable with his mood and swiftly so, ranging rapidly from cold killer gray to hot and angry green and even to glowing gold. Men watched his eyes as cattle brokers watch the ticker tape. Their shade was the only thing by which it was possible to predict Kit Gordon's next move.

The men who told stories of him would have been shocked to have seen him now. They stressed the meticulousness of his clothes, the polish of his sixty-dollar boots, the hang of his black broadcloth coat, the set of his expensive John B.

But their description was inaccurate now. Kit's hands were blistering under the onslaught of the savage sun. His coat was white with alkali dust and the Stetson punctured by a rifle bullet. One of his boots had been scuffed beyond repair when his horse had collapsed under him.

His even-featured face was gray with pain and hunger. He was dying and he knew it. But he was not afraid, only annoyed by the circumstances which had led him to such a pass, at his own foolhardy pursuit of Kettle-Belly Plummer and the flight from the lynch mob in the north.

He was still mystified at the rapidity of his downfall, angered by the injustice which had been done.

Two hundred miles north, at the Santa Fe whistling post of Randall, his hotel room had been looted in his absence and his change of clothing had vanished. A private inquiry had elicited the information that the gunman named Plummer, an enemy of old standing, had been seen in the vicinity. Kit Gordon had preferred to do his own justice, had taken the trail.

But he had found no trace of Kettle-Belly Plummer though he had searched for two days in the surrounding country. He would not have cared about the suit and hat and boots. But among the loot had been a repeater watch, a favored possession and good-luck piece worth around a thousand dollars. That watch had once been the property of Kettle-Belly Plummer until that unworthy had lost it across the faro table in Dodge, two years before. In the following fight, Kit Gordon had kept the watch.

Trying to think of some way to get a line on the obvious thief, Kit had returned to Randall, intending to press his inquiry even further. His reception was amazing.

The town marshal, backed by a mob of railroad workers, had tried to arrest him and Kit, knowing a lynch mob when he saw one, had resisted. Before the marshal and two section hands had thumped into the dust of the street, Kit Gordon had been hit and hit hard with a bullet in his right shoulder but he had managed to escape.

The only intelligence he had of the affair was that he had been *seen* leading the gang which had stopped and robbed the Limited the night before, dynamiting the express car and killing a messenger.

Kit knew the answer to that. Plummer was settling the score in his own back-knifing way. If Kit could only find Plummer . . .

His tongue swelling in his mouth from thirst, with hanging behind him and torturous death at hand, he lay exhausted, watching the maddening mirages come and go, growing palm trees and spouting fountains from the caustic sand. A train puffed importantly where a train would never run. A town fried a hundred feet in the air.

The town was what interested Kit. It was certainly somewhere near at hand or else it could not have its picture projected upon the shimmering sky in that ridiculous fashion.

His head felt light and through it ran the crazy string of his thoughts. He considered the town with a practiced eye, even amused when it occurred to him that he was inspecting something which was probably a hundred miles away and far beyond the normal range of sight.

He could read the signs very clearly. The Bird Cage Opera House. The *Seco Hombre* Saloon. Wells Fargo's stage was drawn up before the post office and the citizens were standing about.

As is the trick of the mirage at times, all things were greatly magnified so that the men and horses appeared ten times their usual size.

One fellow in particular attracted Kit Gordon's attention. The man was very tall and thickly built, with a black beard and a black hat. He hovered on the rim of the crowd as though he did not want to be seen and then, abruptly, turned on his heel and sprinted for a horse.

With one foot in the stirrup, he started to mount. The men in the crowd seemed to be very agitated as they started toward him on the run.

And then, as is the habit of the mirage, having started the drama it refused to longer amuse Kit Gordon by completing it. Empty air writhed with heat waves and the town was gone.

To find out more about *King of the Gunmen* and how you can obtain your copy, go to www.goldenagestories.com.

Glossary

Glossary

STORIES FROM THE GOLDEN AGE *reflect the words and expressions used in the 1930s and 1940s, adding unique flavor and authenticity to the tales. While a character's speech may often reflect regional origins, it also can convey attitudes common in the day. So that readers can better grasp such cultural and historical terms, uncommon words or expressions of the era, the following glossary has been provided.*

---

alkali: a powdery white mineral that salts the ground in many low places in the West. It whitens the ground where water has risen to the surface and gone back down.

arroyo: (chiefly in southwestern US) a small, steep-sided watercourse or gulch with a nearly flat floor, usually dry except after heavy rains.

barbiquejo: (Spanish) chin strap.

batwings: long chaps (leather leggings the cowboy wears to protect his legs) with big flaps of leather. They usually fasten with rings and snaps.

Bird Cage Opera House: a combination saloon, gambling hall and brothel. The name was a fancy way in the 1880s of describing such a place.

boot: saddle boot; a close-fitting covering or case for a gun or other weapon that straps to a saddle.

Boot Hill: a cemetery in a settlement on the US frontier, especially one for gunfighters killed in action. It was given its name because most of its early occupants died with their boots on.

box: the driver's seat on a wagon.

brand artist: a rustler, one expert at changing brands.

buckaroo: a cowboy of the West known for great horsemanship and horse-training techniques. Buckaroos distinguish themselves by their open-crowned hats with short flat brims, silk scarves, chinks (shorter leather chaps), high-heeled boots, dark wool vests and white, long-sleeved, button-down shirts.

buscadero belt: a broad belt for two guns, one on either side.

button: a young person; youth.

caboosed: jailed.

California hat: a soft felt broad-brimmed hat.

Californy: California rig; a one-cinched saddle on a California tree. A tree is the wooden frame of the saddle that is covered with leather. The saddle usually takes its name from the shape of its tree, indicating where it was made.

casita: (Spanish) a small house.

caterwauling: making a harsh, disagreeable noise that sounds like the cry of cats.

cavvy: the herd of saddle horses from which ranch hands select their mounts.

chuck: food.

chuck wagon: a mess wagon of the cow country. It is usually made by fitting, at the back end of an ordinary farm wagon, a large box that contains shelves and has a hinged lid fitted with legs that serves as a table when lowered. The chuck wagon is a cowboy's home on the range, where he keeps his bedroll and dry clothes, gets his food and has a warm fire.

chute: a passage between fences or rails, sometimes narrowing, in which horses or cattle are driven into rodeo arenas, corrals, etc.

Colt: a single-action, six-shot cylinder revolver, most commonly available in .45- or .44-caliber versions. It was first manufactured in 1873 for the Army by the Colt Firearms Company, the armory founded by American inventor Samuel Colt (1814–1862) who revolutionized the firearms industry with the invention of the revolver. The Colt, also known as the Peacemaker, was also made available to civilians. As a reliable, inexpensive and popular handgun among cowboys, it became known as the "cowboy's gun" and a symbol of the Old West.

concentrate: the desired mineral that is left after impurities have been removed from mined ore.

coyote: used for a man who has the sneaking and skulking characteristics of a coyote.

crawl leather: to mount a horse's saddle.

cripes: used as a mild oath or an exclamation of astonishment.

Derringer: a pocket-sized, short-barreled, large-caliber pistol. Named for the US gunsmith Henry Deringer (1786–1868), who designed it.

'dobe: short for adobe; a building constructed with sun-dried bricks made from clay.

'dobe wallin': adobe walling; standing one against an adobe wall and executing by shooting. An adobe building is constructed of sun-dried bricks made from clay.

down at the heels: shabby; rundown; poor.

dry-gulch: to kill; ambush.

fanning: firing a series of shots (from a single-action revolver) by holding the trigger back and successively striking the hammer to the rear with the free hand.

faro: a gambling game played with cards and popular in the American West of the nineteenth century. In faro, the players bet on the order in which the cards will be turned over by the dealer. The cards were kept in a dealing box to keep track of the play.

figger: figure.

forefooted: roping an animal by the forefeet. A bronc roped by the neck is more likely to be injured and to fight back as he thinks his life is at stake. Forefooting is preferable and helps to convince the bronc that a man can and will handle him without much trouble and that the man is not trying to kill him.

G-men: government men; agents of the Federal Bureau of Investigation.

green-gilled: green around the gills; to be pale or sickly in appearance from nervousness or from being frightened.

gunhawk: a wandering gunfighter.

hackamore: a halter with reins and a noseband instead of a bit (a metal bar that fits into the horse's mouth and attaches to the reins), used for breaking horses and riding.

halter broke: trained to run with the remuda (saddle horses from which ranch hands pick mounts for the day).

hazed: 1. rode alongside a bronc and kept it from running into obstructions while the bronc buster tries to break it. 2. drove (as cattle or horses) from horseback.

Hickok: James Butler Hickok, better known as Wild Bill Hickok (1837–1876), a legendary figure in the American Old West. After fighting in the Union Army during the Civil War, he became a famous Army scout and, later, lawman and gunfighter.

hombre: a man, especially in the Southwest. Sometimes it implies a rough fellow, a tough; often it means a real man.

hoss: horse.

iron: a handgun, especially a revolver.

John B.: Stetson.

Kansas toothpick: variation of Arkansas toothpick; a large sheath knife; a dagger.

látigo: a long strap on a Western saddle, used to adjust the cinch.

Limited: a train line making only a limited number of stops en route. The full name for the line was often abbreviated down to simply *Limited.*

line camp: an outpost cabin, tent or dugout that serves as a base of operations where line riders are housed. *Line riders* are cowboys that follow a ranch's fences or boundaries and maintain order along the borders of a cattleman's property, such as looking after stock, etc.

lit: got off (a horse).

lucifer: a match.

lynch mob: a group of people who capture and hang someone without legal arrest and trial, because they think the person has committed a crime.

mesquite: any of several small spiny trees or shrubs native to the southwestern US and Mexico, and important as plants for bees and forage for cattle.

Navvy rugs: Navajo rug; Navajo weavers produced textiles that were extraordinary in terms of weave and design.

needle gun: Dreyse needle gun; a rifle used on the frontier and called this because of its 0.5-inch needlelike firing pin that detonates the powder by plunging through the paper cartridge to strike the primer at the base of the bullet. It was invented by the gunsmith Johann Nikolaus von Dreyse (1787–1867).

outlaw: a wild or vicious horse.

owl-hoot: outlaw; a lawless person.

papoose: a Native American infant or very young child.

plugs: worthless horses.

prickly pear: a cactus with flattened, jointed, spiny stems and pear-shaped fruits that are edible in some species.

puncher: a hired hand who tends cattle and performs other duties on horseback.

quirly: a cigarette that is rolled by hand.

quirt: a riding whip with a short handle and a braided leather lash.

ramrod: a foreman; a superintendent.

rannies: ranahans; cowboys or top ranch hands.

repeater watch: a pocket watch that chimes every one, twelve or twenty-four hours.

riata: a long noosed rope used to catch animals.

rimfire: a saddle with one cinch that is placed far to the front; also called a *Spanish rig* or *rimmy.*

rotgut: raw, inferior liquor.

saddle tramp: a professional chuck-line (food-line) rider; anyone who is out of a job and riding through the country. Any worthy cowboy may be forced to ride chuck-line at certain seasons, but the professional chuck-line rider is just a plain range bum, despised by all cowboys. He is one who takes advantage of the country's hospitality and stays as long as he dares wherever there is no work for him to do and the meals are free and regular.

Scheherazade: the female narrator of *The Arabian Nights,* who during one thousand and one adventurous nights saved her life by entertaining her husband, the king, with stories.

Seco Hombre: (Spanish) dry man. Used here as the name of a saloon.

sheep-eye: to look at wishfully.

sougan: bedroll; a blanket or quilt with a protective canvas tarp for use on a bunk or on the range.

sowbelly: salt pork; pork cured in salt, especially fatty pork from the back, side or belly of a hog.

spring holster: a holster that permits the user to take the gun from it quickly by pulling out instead of up.

spring wagon: a light farm wagon equipped with springs.

Stetson: as the most popular broad-brimmed hat in the West, it became the generic name for *hat*. John B. Stetson was a master hat maker and founder of the company that has been making Stetsons since 1865. Not only can the Stetson stand up to a terrific amount of beating, the cowboy's hat has more different uses than any other garment he wears. It keeps the sun out of the eyes and off the neck; it serves as an umbrella; it makes a great fan, which sometimes is needed when building a fire or shunting cattle about; the brim serves as a cup to water oneself, or as a bucket to water the horse or put out the fire.

sunfish: a way of bucking; the horse throws its middle violently to one side, then the other, so that it seems its shoulder may touch the ground, letting the sunlight hit its belly.

ten-spot: a ten-dollar bill.

Texas fever: a fever caused by ticks and spread by the immune but tick-infested cattle of the southern country to cattle of more northern latitudes. The prevalence of this fever was greatly responsible for stopping the old trail drives.

thirteen steps: gallows; traditionally, there are thirteen steps leading up to a gallows.

thunderation: an exclamation of annoyance or surprise.

vaquero: (Spanish) a cowboy or herdsman.

waddy: a cowboy, especially one who drifts from ranch to ranch and helps out in busy times. In the spring and fall when some ranches were short-handed, they took on anyone who was able to ride a horse and used him for a week or so; hence the word *waddy,* derived from *wadding*—anything to fill in. Some cowmen used the word to mean a cattle rustler; later it was applied to any cowboy.

war bag or **war sack:** a cowboy's bag for his personal possessions, plunder, cartridges, etc. Often made of canvas but sometimes just a flour or grain sack and usually tied behind the saddle.

whang leather: tough leather adapted for strings, thongs, belt-lacing, etc., commonly made from calf hide.

whistling post: whistle stop; a small town or community.

Winchester: an early family of repeating rifles; a single-barreled rifle containing multiple rounds of ammunition. Manufactured by the Winchester Repeating Arms Company, it was widely used in the US during the latter half of the nineteenth century. The 1873 model is often called "the gun that won the West" for its immense popularity at that time, as well as its use in fictional Westerns.

wrangler: a cowboy who takes care of the saddle horses.

L. Ron Hubbard
in the Golden Age
of Pulp Fiction

*In writing an adventure story
a writer has to know that he is adventuring
for a lot of people who cannot.
The writer has to take them here and there
about the globe and show them
excitement and love and realism.
As long as that writer is living the part of an
adventurer when he is hammering
the keys, he is succeeding with his story.*

*Adventuring is a state of mind.
If you adventure through life, you have a
good chance to be a success on paper.*

*Adventure doesn't mean globe-trotting,
exactly, and it doesn't mean great deeds.
Adventuring is like art.
You have to live it to make it real.*

—*L. RON HUBBARD*

L. Ron Hubbard
and American
Pulp Fiction

B ORN March 13, 1911, L. Ron Hubbard lived a life at
least as expansive as the stories with which he enthralled
a hundred million readers through a fifty-year career.

Originally hailing from Tilden, Nebraska, he spent his
formative years in a classically rugged Montana, replete with
the cowpunchers, lawmen and desperadoes who would later
people his Wild West adventures. And lest anyone imagine
those adventures were drawn from vicarious experience, he
was not only breaking broncs at a tender age, he was also
among the few whites ever admitted into Blackfoot society
as a bona fide blood brother. While if only to round out an
otherwise rough and tumble youth, his mother was that rarity
of her time—a thoroughly educated woman—who introduced
her son to the classics of Occidental literature even before his
seventh birthday.

But as any dedicated L. Ron Hubbard reader will attest, his
world extended far beyond Montana. In point of fact, and as the
son of a United States naval officer, by the age of eighteen he
had traveled over a quarter of a million miles. Included therein
were three Pacific crossings to a then still mysterious Asia, where
he ran with the likes of Her British Majesty's agent-in-place

L. Ron Hubbard, left, at Congressional Airport, Washington, DC, 1931, with members of George Washington University flying club.

for North China, and the last in the line of Royal Magicians from the court of Kublai Khan. For the record, L. Ron Hubbard was also among the first Westerners to gain admittance to forbidden Tibetan monasteries below Manchuria, and his photographs of China's Great Wall long graced American geography texts.

Upon his return to the United States and a hasty completion of his interrupted high school education, the young Ron Hubbard entered George Washington University. There, as fans of his aerial adventures may have heard, he earned his wings as a pioneering barnstormer at the dawn of American aviation. He also earned a place in free-flight record books for the longest sustained flight above Chicago. Moreover, as a roving reporter for *Sportsman Pilot* (featuring his first professionally penned articles), he further helped inspire a generation of pilots who would take America to world airpower.

Immediately beyond his sophomore year, Ron embarked on the first of his famed ethnological expeditions, initially to then untrammeled Caribbean shores (descriptions of which would later fill a whole series of West Indies mystery-thrillers). That the Puerto Rican interior would also figure into the future of Ron Hubbard stories was likewise no accident. For in addition to cultural studies of the island, a 1932–33

LRH expedition is rightly remembered as conducting the first complete mineralogical survey of a Puerto Rico under United States jurisdiction.

There was many another adventure along this vein: As a lifetime member of the famed Explorers Club, L. Ron Hubbard charted North Pacific waters with the first shipboard radio direction finder, and so pioneered a long-range navigation system universally employed until the late twentieth century. While not to put too fine an edge on it, he also held a rare Master Mariner's license to pilot any vessel, of any tonnage in any ocean.

Yet lest we stray too far afield, there is an LRH note at this juncture in his saga, and it reads in part:

"I started out writing for the pulps, writing the best I knew, writing for every mag on the stands, slanting as well as I could."

To which one might add: His earliest submissions date from the summer of 1934, and included tales drawn from true-to-life Asian adventures, with characters roughly modeled on British/American intelligence operatives he had known in Shanghai. His early Westerns were similarly peppered with details drawn from personal experience. Although therein lay a first hard lesson from the often cruel world of the pulps. His first Westerns were soundly rejected as lacking the authenticity of a Max Brand yarn

Capt. L. Ron Hubbard in Ketchikan, Alaska, 1940, on his Alaskan Radio Experimental Expedition, the first of three voyages conducted under the Explorers Club flag.

(a particularly frustrating comment given L. Ron Hubbard's Westerns came straight from his Montana homeland, while Max Brand was a mediocre New York poet named Frederick Schiller Faust, who turned out implausible six-shooter tales from the terrace of an Italian villa).

Nevertheless, and needless to say, L. Ron Hubbard persevered and soon earned a reputation as among the most publishable names in pulp fiction, with a ninety percent placement rate of first-draft manuscripts. He was also among the most prolific, averaging between seventy and a hundred thousand words a month. Hence the rumors that L. Ron Hubbard had redesigned a typewriter for faster keyboard action and pounded out manuscripts on a continuous roll of butcher paper to save the precious seconds it took to insert a single sheet of paper into manual typewriters of the day.

That all L. Ron Hubbard stories did not run beneath said byline is yet another aspect of pulp fiction lore. That is, as publishers periodically rejected manuscripts from top-drawer authors if only to avoid paying top dollar, L. Ron Hubbard and company just as frequently replied with submissions under various pseudonyms. In Ron's case, the list

A MAN OF MANY NAMES

Between 1934 and 1950, L. Ron Hubbard authored more than fifteen million words of fiction in more than two hundred classic publications. To supply his fans and editors with stories across an array of genres and pulp titles, he adopted fifteen pseudonyms in addition to his already renowned L. Ron Hubbard byline.

Winchester Remington Colt
Lt. Jonathan Daly
Capt. Charles Gordon
Capt. L. Ron Hubbard
Bernard Hubbel
Michael Keith
Rene Lafayette
Legionnaire 148
Legionnaire 14830
Ken Martin
Scott Morgan
Lt. Scott Morgan
Kurt von Rachen
Barry Randolph
Capt. Humbert Reynolds

included: Rene Lafayette, Captain
Charles Gordon, Lt. Scott Morgan
and the notorious Kurt von
Rachen—supposedly on the lam
for a murder rap, while hammering
out two-fisted prose in Argentina.
The point: While L. Ron Hubbard
as Ken Martin spun stories of
Southeast Asian intrigue, LRH as
Barry Randolph authored tales of

*L. Ron Hubbard,
circa 1930, at the
outset of a literary
career that would
finally span half a
century.*

romance on the Western range—which, stretching
between a dozen genres is how he came to stand
among the two hundred elite authors providing
close to a million tales through the glory days of
American Pulp Fiction.

In evidence of exactly that, by 1936 L. Ron Hubbard was
literally leading pulp fiction's elite as president of New York's
American Fiction Guild. Members included a veritable
pulp hall of fame: Lester "Doc Savage" Dent, Walter "The
Shadow" Gibson, and the legendary Dashiell Hammett—to
cite but a few.

Also in evidence of just where L. Ron Hubbard stood
within his first two years on the American pulp circuit: By the
spring of 1937, he was ensconced in Hollywood, adopting a
Caribbean thriller for Columbia Pictures, remembered today as
The Secret of Treasure Island. Comprising fifteen thirty-minute
episodes, the L. Ron Hubbard screenplay led to the most
profitable matinée serial in Hollywood history. In accord
with Hollywood culture, he was thereafter continually called

The 1937 Secret of Treasure Island, *a fifteen-episode serial adapted for the screen by L. Ron Hubbard from his novel,* Murder at Pirate Castle.

upon to rewrite/doctor scripts—most famously for long-time friend and fellow adventurer Clark Gable.

In the interim—and herein lies another distinctive chapter of the L. Ron Hubbard story—he continually worked to open Pulp Kingdom gates to up-and-coming authors. Or, for that matter, anyone who wished to write. It was a fairly unconventional stance, as markets were already thin and competition razor sharp. But the fact remains, it was an L. Ron Hubbard hallmark that he vehemently lobbied on behalf of young authors—regularly supplying instructional articles to trade journals, guest-lecturing to short story classes at George Washington University and Harvard, and even founding his own creative writing competition. It was established in 1940, dubbed the Golden Pen, and guaranteed winners both New York representation and publication in *Argosy*.

But it was John W. Campbell Jr.'s *Astounding Science Fiction* that finally proved the most memorable LRH vehicle. While every fan of L. Ron Hubbard's galactic epics undoubtedly knows the story, it nonetheless bears repeating: By late 1938, the pulp publishing magnate of Street & Smith was determined to revamp *Astounding Science Fiction* for broader readership. In particular, senior editorial director F. Orlin Tremaine called for stories with a stronger *human element*. When acting editor John W. Campbell balked, preferring his spaceship-driven tales,

Tremaine enlisted Hubbard. Hubbard, in turn, replied with the genre's first truly *character-driven* works, wherein heroes are pitted not against bug-eyed monsters but the mystery and majesty of deep space itself—and thus was launched the Golden Age of Science Fiction.

The names alone are enough to quicken the pulse of any science fiction aficionado, including LRH friend and protégé, Robert Heinlein, Isaac Asimov, A. E. van Vogt and Ray Bradbury. Moreover, when coupled with LRH stories of fantasy, we further come to what's rightly been described as the

foundation of every modern tale of horror: L. Ron Hubbard's immortal *Fear*. It was rightly proclaimed by Stephen King as one of the very few works to genuinely warrant that overworked term "classic"—as in: *"This is a classic tale of creeping, surreal menace and horror. . . . This is one of the really, really good ones."*

L. Ron Hubbard, 1948, among fellow science fiction luminaries at the World Science Fiction Convention in Toronto.

To accommodate the greater body of L. Ron Hubbard fantasies, Street & Smith inaugurated *Unknown*—a classic pulp if there ever was one, and wherein readers were soon thrilling to the likes of *Typewriter in the Sky* and *Slaves of Sleep* of which Frederik Pohl would declare: *"There are bits and pieces from Ron's work that became part of the language in ways that very few other writers managed."*

And, indeed, at J. W. Campbell Jr.'s insistence, Ron was regularly drawing on themes from the Arabian Nights and so introducing readers to a world of genies, jinn, Aladdin and Sinbad—all of which, of course, continue to float through cultural mythology to this day.

At least as influential in terms of post-apocalypse stories was L. Ron Hubbard's 1940 *Final Blackout*. Generally acclaimed as the finest anti-war novel of the decade and among the ten best works of the genre ever authored—here, too, was a tale that would live on in ways few other writers

imagined. Hence, the later Robert Heinlein verdict: "Final Blackout *is as perfect a piece of science fiction as has ever been written.*"

Like many another who both lived and wrote American pulp adventure, the war proved a tragic end to Ron's sojourn in the pulps. He served with distinction in four theaters and was highly decorated for commanding corvettes in the North Pacific. He was also grievously wounded in combat, lost many a close friend and colleague and thus resolved to say farewell to pulp fiction and devote himself to what it had supported these many years—namely, his serious research.

Portland, Oregon, 1943; L. Ron Hubbard captain of the US Navy subchaser PC 815.

But in no way was the LRH literary saga at an end, for as he wrote some thirty years later, in 1980:

"Recently there came a period when I had little to do. This was novel in a life so crammed with busy years, and I decided to amuse myself by writing a novel that was pure science fiction."

That work was *Battlefield Earth: A Saga of the Year 3000*. It was an immediate *New York Times* bestseller and, in fact, the first international science fiction blockbuster in decades. It was not, however, L. Ron Hubbard's magnum opus, as that distinction is generally reserved for his next and final work: The 1.2 million word *Mission Earth*.

> **Final Blackout**
> *is as perfect*
> *a piece of*
> *science fiction as*
> *has ever*
> *been written.*
>
> —Robert Heinlein

How he managed those 1.2 million words in just over twelve months is yet another piece of the L. Ron Hubbard legend. But the fact remains, he did indeed author a ten-volume *dekalogy* that lives in publishing history for the fact that each and every volume of the series was also a *New York Times* bestseller.

Moreover, as subsequent generations discovered L. Ron Hubbard through republished works and novelizations of his screenplays, the mere fact of his name on a cover signaled an international bestseller. . . . Until, to date, sales of his works exceed hundreds of millions, and he otherwise remains among the most enduring and widely read authors in literary history. Although as a final word on the tales of L. Ron Hubbard, perhaps it's enough to simply reiterate what editors told readers in the glory days of American Pulp Fiction:

He writes the way he does, brothers, because he's been there, seen it and done it!

THE STORIES FROM THE GOLDEN AGE

Your ticket to adventure starts here with the Stories from
the Golden Age collection by master storyteller L. Ron Hubbard.
These gripping tales are set in a kaleidoscope of exotic locales and brim
with fascinating characters, including some of the
most vile villains, dangerous dames and brazen heroes
you'll ever get to meet.

The entire collection of over one hundred and fifty stories is being
released in a series of eighty books and audiobooks.
For an up-to-date listing of available titles,
go to www.goldenagestories.com.

AIR ADVENTURE

Arctic Wings	*Man-Killers of the Air*
The Battling Pilot	*On Blazing Wings*
Boomerang Bomber	*Red Death Over China*
The Crate Killer	*Sabotage in the Sky*
The Dive Bomber	*Sky Birds Dare!*
Forbidden Gold	*The Sky-Crasher*
Hurtling Wings	*Trouble on His Wings*
The Lieutenant Takes the Sky	*Wings Over Ethiopia*

FAR-FLUNG ADVENTURE

SEA ADVENTURE

TALES FROM THE ORIENT

MYSTERY

135

FANTASY

SCIENCE FICTION

WESTERN

JOIN THE PULP REVIVAL
America in the 1930s and 40s

Pulp fiction was in its heyday and 30 million readers were regularly riveted by the larger-than-life tales of master storyteller L. Ron Hubbard. For this was pulp fiction's golden age, when the writing was raw and every page packed a walloping punch.

That magic can now be yours. An evocative world of nefarious villains, exotic intrigues, courageous heroes and heroines—a world that today's cinema has barely tapped for tales of adventure and swashbucklers.

Enroll today in the Stories from the Golden Age Club and begin receiving your monthly feature edition selected from more than 150 stories in the collection.

You may choose to enjoy them as either a paperback or audiobook for the special membership price of $9.95 each month along with FREE shipping and handling.

CALL TOLL-FREE: **1-877-8GALAXY**
(1-877-842-5299) OR GO ONLINE TO
www.goldenagestories.com
AND BECOME PART OF THE PULP REVIVAL!

Prices are set in US dollars only. For non-US residents, please call
1-323-466-7815 for pricing information. Free shipping available for US residents only.

Galaxy Press, 7051 Hollywood Blvd., Suite 200, Hollywood, CA 90028